Champagne &
Forever

A Country Road Novella

Michelle—
Love and Friendship
Forever
Andrea Johnston

andrea johnston

Champagne & Forever
(A Country Road Novella – Book 3.5)

Copyright © 2017 by Andrea Johnston

Cover Photo: iStock

Cover design by Uplifting Designs
www.uplifting-designs.com

Editing by Karen L. of The Proof Is in the Reading, LLC

Interior design by Stacey Blake of Champagne Book Design
champagnebookdesign.com

First Edition
ISBN-13: 978-1979263184

Dedication

For Kiersten
Because life is better with good champagne
and amazing friends.

Champagne & Forever

October 21

Wedding Day

"Uhh . . . Ben?"

I hear Landon calling me from the hallway bathroom. His voice is higher than usual and slightly panicked. I look over at my best man, Jameson, who slinks down in Piper's reading chair, drinking straight from a bottle of Jägermeister while one of my groomsmen, Owen, looks at his phone, smiling. Neither of them seem interested in whatever Landon's emergency is from the other room. I'll be honest, going into the bathroom to see what Landon needs is low on my list of things to do today. I'm getting married in a little over an hour, and I'm more concerned with why this damn shirt is fucking twisted under my vest than anything else.

"What's up?" I ask, walking out of my bedroom toward Landon's shouting. Damn this vest. I swear to God, if I didn't love Piper and plan on making her Mrs. Sullivan in . . . fifty-eight minutes, I'd rip this damn vest off and burn it like some sort of sacrificial lamb. I stand in the doorway adjusting myself as Landon keeps his back to me, not moving, and looking toward his shoes.

I follow Landon's gaze to his feet and still don't see the problem. No water on the floor, no trash spilled anywhere. Nothing out of the ordinary. Of course, we're all dressed to the nines in these rented suits but otherwise, we're just four buddies waiting for a party. I guess it's a little more than a party, but still, other than the matching black suits and fancy ties—mine is silver, or shimmery gray as Piper called it, and theirs are a deep purple color to match the bridesmaids' dresses. Yet, Landon continues to stand in front of me, like a damn statue.

"Dude," I say while finally giving up on this damn shirt.

"Do you have something to say?" Landon asks as he turns to me with a six-inch piece of plastic hanging from his fingers. I notice he is using a piece of tissue to hold the thing between his fingers.

It's hours . . . okay, maybe seconds, between Landon asking me if I have something to say and me realizing what he's holding in his hands.

A pregnancy test.

"Oh fuck!" My voice is not calm and it most definitely isn't subdued. Nope. I fucking yelled that like we were in a large room and every person was hard of hearing.

"What?" Jameson shouts from his perch.

"Did you rip your shirt with all that tugging? Piper will kill you," Owen warns. *Don't I know it.*

"Uh . . ." I'm not often at a loss for words, but right

now? Yeah, I don't have many. Before I can offer an ex-
planation, I hear the gasps of horror behind me as both
Jameson and Owen hover.

"Not it!"

"Not it!"

Jameson and Owen shout in unison.

"Fuck you guys!" Seems like a logical response from
me to them on my wedding day.

"Uh, guys? Who has an announcement to make?"
Landon asks while completely calm, cool, and collected.
Of course, he is. He's fucking single and not possibly a dad.

I could be a dad!

I.

Could.

Be.

A *DAD!*

This isn't the plan. Sure, it's something we've talked about and the more I think about it, the less freaked
out I am. Fuck it, I'm excited at the possibility. A million
thoughts swarm my mind. What if the minute I make
Piper my wife, I also find out she's the mother of my child?
The thought makes me smile like a goddamn cat that ate
the canary. Fuck, this is it. This is everything I've wanted.
To marry Piper Lawrence and make a family with her.

"Shit," Jameson says, rubbing a hand down his face.
"I swear it was that one time. Goddammit." I watch as he
walks away and throws himself onto Piper's reading chair
in the corner. His dramatics indicate he's been spending far
too much time with my sister, Ashton, also his girlfriend.

"I know I've wrapped it, plus Min is on the pill. We're

double covered. Like *Madea* would say, 'Ain't nobody got time for this shit,'" Owen declares like he's calling out a new bill in Congress.

"I'm not sure that's what *Madea* says. But regardless, someone is pregnant, and the last people in this room were the girls." I know this to be true because Piper and the girls were here Thursday night but stayed at Jameson and Ashton's last night to make sure I didn't see her before the wedding. And to keep Piper from going to full-blown bridezilla.

That means either my fiancée, my sister, or one of my best friends' girlfriend is pregnant. Really, if my sister is pregnant, it also means my best friend's girlfriend is pregnant. Shit. This day just got a lot more complicated than any of us planned.

A very Biper wedding this is—chaos, confusion, and a whole lot of love.

A baby is coming, and we're all going to change because of it.

Ben & Piper

One week before the wedding day

Chapter 1

Ben

I love watching Piper sleep. Sometimes I wonder if I border on the line of creeper status instead of undying love. She is a sound sleeper, often waking in the same position she falls asleep in. Lying on her side, her hands are tucked under her chin, pulling her pillow into herself like she's cuddling, and her knee lifted so, if she wanted to, she could knee me in the balls. Her face is void of makeup, and her freckles dance across her skin. I love watching her eyelids dance as she dreams, but it's the way she smiles at me as she wakes that takes my breath away. Her expression is full of love and happiness. Well, and confirmation I am one hundred percent entering creeper status.

"You are such a weirdo." Her voice is raspy and unfiltered. I love it. My hand slides across her belly to her side. Slowly making my way up her sides to her breasts, I smile as I lower my lips to her neck. A nibble here and a lick there sends visible shivers across Piper's skin.

"I'm your weirdo, though." My voice is equally raspy. I love this, how raw we are in the morning. Piper is uninhibited and unfiltered. Her thoughts are natural and without the worry or stress of our upcoming wedding clouding them. These moments, when it's only us, they are what we're about. The rest is just window dressing to the life we're building. I'm grateful for our quiet mornings before the chaos begins. As elementary school teachers, we're pulled in so many different directions each day, it's a wonder we've managed to plan this wedding. In seven days this amazing woman will be my wife. Sure, it was a tough sell in the beginning, but I knew the minute I saw her: Piper Lawrence was going to change my life.

Okay, so maybe not the first time I saw her.

Or, for the next eighteen . . . or twenty years. Okay fine, I didn't notice. Not because she wasn't amazing or beautiful then. No, because I was a fucking jackass and completely blinded by things I didn't know I needed. But here we are. Together and happy. Engaged.

Piper turned my life upside down, and for that I'm eternally grateful. Her smile, her giggle, and her love of the ugliest leggings made me stop and evaluate my life over the past year. The night I saw her waving her arms like a maniac at Country Road, I knew I had to get to know her. The moment my lips met hers, that zing or zang, whatever people say you feel, was immediate. I had no way of knowing how much the feisty and animated beauty talking to my sister would change me and the course of my life.

All for the better.

Piper Lawrence is kind, smart, and beautiful, but above it all . . . she's mine. I move my hand to her breast, thumbing her nipple as it hardens. I watch as she smiles ever so slightly as I rub light circles over the hardening peak. Before she can release the little whimper she grants me most mornings, I capture the nipple between my lips, flicking it with my tongue. Piper's hands go to my hair and run through the too long locks before tugging. It's why I keep it a little long—the tug.

This is type of morning sex that doesn't require me to play with her. I don't need to slip my finger under her panties. I don't need to flick her clit, and I don't need to lick my way down to her sweet spot. No, this morning Piper is ready for me. Like so many others in the last ten months we've lived together, I'm able to simply tug her panties down and push into her. I feel her walls tighten as she captures me, her hands pull me closer as I grip her hips and pull her to me, thrust by thrust.

"Oh . . . my . . . gawd . . . Ben . . ."

I love hearing her struggle for words. It fuels me as I quickly, too quickly, bring her with me to the edge. Swiftly, and with the precision of a man who knows how to make his woman explode, I pump once then twice before Piper arches her back and I feel her grip me like a vice. I immediately follow, my moans loud and animalistic.

"Mmm, good morning," Piper coos as she kisses me gently on the lips and smiles, her eyes still closed.

"Morning, baby."

I pull from Piper and plant a quick kiss to her lips before smacking her on the ass as she rolls to her side, pacified. I tread into the master bathroom and turn on the shower. While the water warms, I toss a towel toward Piper; it lands on the bed in front of her. She smiles, never opening her eyes, and pulls the towel under the covers and between her legs. I'm stepping in the shower when I hear her shout something about coffee and breakfast. Her words are muffled as I lean my head under the water.

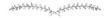

After breakfast, Piper and I handled a few house chores before packing our bags for the night. With our wedding taking place on our property, there is a little chaos around the house. My man cave, originally a formal dining room, has been transformed into a staging area for all things wedding. I've seen more of my mom and Piper's mom in the last three weeks than the last six months combined.

When we decided to keep the wedding small and intimate and more of a party than anything else, I didn't realize how much work would go into it. Some days I think I should have convinced Piper to elope to a tropical island somewhere. We'd already be married and lying in the sun if I had my say. But, I don't. I'm the groom, and I live to make my bride happy. She wants a wedding, and a wedding we will have.

My dad has been working on the arbor we'll stand under for the ceremony for a few months. He hasn't let either of us see it, but my mom promises it's beautiful and when the wedding is over, we will be able to put it in the garden where Piper has a little table and chairs set up. A table and chairs nobody sits on. I don't ask. Again, whatever my bride wants.

"Babe, do you know where my anti-frizz serum is?"

"Piper, why would I know where that is? I don't use hair products."

"Ben." She sighs. It's a sweet sigh with a smile as she approaches me. Once her hands wrap around my waist, I mimic her move, tug her to me, and lower my lips to hers. After a few dozen kisses that leave her panting, I pull away and allow her to continue speaking. Instead, Piper stands before me, her eyes closed and her lips lifted to a smirk.

"You had something to say, babe?"

"Huh? Oh, yeah. How do you do that?"

"What's that?" I ask as I walk to the refrigerator and pull out a bottle of water, opening it and quickly finishing half of it off in one gulp.

"Kiss me stupid. I know I had a question, but you do that and I forget my own name."

"Piper Sullivan."

"Gosh, I love when you say that." Piper walks up to me and steals the bottle of water from my hands, taking her own sip before handing it back to me.

"Only seven days. Anyway, you were asking about hair products. I don't know where any of that is, but if it's a serum, my sister probably has it. Witchy powers and all that," I tease.

Piper smacks my arm, which causes me to fake a flinch and turn my back toward her as though I'm protecting myself. "Be nice; that's my best friend you're making fun of."

"Oh, come on. If I can't make fun of my own sister, what's the point of having her? Besides, you know she's been a little on edge lately. More so than usual. Are you sure we should've asked her to sing at the wedding?"

"We didn't ask; she offered. It's her gift to us, and I can't think of anything better than hearing Ashton sing our wedding song to us. Even thinking about it makes me misty-eyed," she says, waving her hands in front of her face. "Dammit. I don't know why I keep crying."

"It's okay," I say, pulling her into a hug. I rest my chin on top of her head as she sniffles. "I love your hormones. As long as they're more like this than the crazy lunatic Ashton has been the last few weeks. And, don't get me started on Minnie. I saw her and Owen at the grocery store the other day and he looked scared to death. The entire cart was chocolate and chips. Poor guy."

"Hey, those are my friends you're mocking. Be kind, Bentley Sullivan." Piper mock smacks me on the chest as I chuckle and tug her back into my chest, wrapping my arms around her.

"I'm sorry, baby. You're right. But I thought that whole, chicks syncing up was a myth. I guess it's not. Speaking of, when are J and Ash supposed to be here? I'm ready to go up to the lake."

"Sounds like they just pulled in. I need to finish packing. Will you send Ash upstairs?" She asks pulling away from me.

"Sure thing, baby. Go on."

Piper takes my water from my hands again, but this time doesn't hand it back. Instead, she takes it with her up the stairs to our room leaving me standing here alone. This is our bachelor and bachelorette weekend. The guys are taking me to Jameson's property to fish, have a bonfire, and drink too much whiskey. The girls have planned an afternoon at a spa and a night of sushi and cocktails before they go back to Jameson and Ashton's house for a sleepover. Knowing the three of them, the sleepover is only an excuse for gossip and more cocktails.

Two quick knocks at the door signal Jameson and Ashton have arrived before I hear the screen creak open. Let the fun begin.

Chapter 2

Piper

Where is my damn anti-frizz serum? I swear I'm losing my mind. The other day, I called one of my students Tommy three times. There is no Tommy in my class. I'd blame it on lack of sleep, but I've been doing nothing but sleeping lately. I'm so freaking tired. This wedding is killing me. I thought I had it all figured out three months ago, but in the last few weeks it's all come to a head, and I realized there's a lot of work that goes into even a small gathering of friends and family.

I hear footsteps on the stairs while I'm on all fours on the floor, looking under our bed for my missing hair product. Sure, a sane person wouldn't think to look here for something that should be in the bathroom. But I found the remote control in the fridge the other day, so I'm not assuming anything at this point.

"What the hell are you doing? Some new yoga shit?

Oh, don't tell me, the Kama Sutra? You and my brother into some kinky shit, Pipe?"

I sigh; Ashton is my very best friend in the world, but I swear some days I don't know where she comes up with this stuff. What do you know, there's my serum. I pull the bottle from under the bed victoriously to find Ashton lying on her stomach on my bed, her feet crossed in the air, her chin resting on her shoulder.

"Whatcha got there? Massage oil? I said spa party, but it's not that kind of happy ending, Piper."

"Oh, shut up. I've been looking for this bottle for hours. I'm not sure why it's under the bed, but I'm glad I didn't throw it away. This stuff is expensive."

I stand and make my way over to the small cosmetics bag on the bathroom counter and toss the bottle in. Once I've looked through the contents and confirmed everything is packed, I return to the bedroom to put the bag in my small suitcase. Ashton is in the same spot, but this time she's crying.

"Ash, what's wrong? Did you and Jameson get in a fight?" I move my suitcase out of the way and sit down in front of her, waiting for a response.

"Of course not. He's amazing. Like the greatest thing ever!" She starts bawling, and I have no idea what is happening.

"You're freaking me out, Ash. What's wrong?"

Before Ashton can respond, Ben shouts to me from the bottom of the stairs that they're ready to leave. I look to Ashton who stands and wipes her eyes with the back of her hand. Two deep breaths and she looks ready to head downstairs. Holy emotional whiplash. Maybe Ben's right, and we should give her an out with singing at the wedding. Obviously, this is too much stress for her.

I follow Ashton down the stairs with my suitcase in one hand and my pillow—Ben's pillow—in the other. Yes, I'm that girl. I haven't slept away from Ben in almost a year. I'm not going to make it through the night without his pillow and his smell. Mock all you want. The guys are standing in the kitchen when we enter. I set my pillow on top of the suitcase and watch as Ashton walks over to Jameson who hoists her up in his arms.

Her feet dangle as he nestles his mouth in the crook of her neck. Ashton lets out a string of giggles, and I smile. A few whispers between them and Ashton nods her head yes as Jameson peppers her with kisses. It took those two a long time to get to where they are, but their story makes me smile. They are truly the epitome of enemies to lovers, my favorite romance trope. It makes my romance loving heart happy to see.

I follow Ashton's lead and walk to Ben's open arms. When Ben takes my face in his hands and gently kisses me, my knees weaken. Growing up, I would dream of Bentley Sullivan. I planned our first date, our courtship, and our wedding. Sure, most of that was when I was eight years old, and I played out each scenario with my Barbies. Now, within a week of our actual wedding, I have to pinch myself to make sure this is happening.

Ben and I hug and kiss a few times before Jameson tugs him away. Ashton and I follow the guys outside and stand on the porch, watching them hop in Jameson's truck.

The minute it rumbles to life, Justin Moore blasts from the speakers, causing Ashton and me to break out in a full force belly laugh. "Point at You" fills the air, and it's absolutely fitting for Jameson and Ashton. For years, Ashton mocked and teased Jameson about his ridiculously raised truck and well-deserved "manwhore" reputation. Regardless of his past and her teasing, she's always been the one to bring him back to reality. Ashton brings out the best in him. When Jameson peels out of our gravel driveway, fishtailing and blowing up a cloud of dust behind him, I roll my eyes and turn to look at Ashton.

"Boys and their toys," Ashton sighs with a smile. I know as much as she does that Jameson could do just about anything and she'd find it endearing.

"I'm all packed. Are you ready to blow this pop stand and pick up Min? I'm so excited for a pedicure it's not even funny!" I say, pulling her from her thoughts.

"You bet your sweet bride-to-be ass. Don't forget our mothers are coming to this portion of the party."

Ashton opens the screen door, motioning for me to enter before her. I fling my purse over my shoulder while simultaneously grabbing my pillow before grasping my suitcase handle. "I told you I was fine having the moms here for the entire night, Ash. Remember, low-key. Nothing will ensure that like having our moms here. Just us with some sparkly toes and lots of margaritas."

"I know, but *you* know I'm a little hard of hearing when you go all Pollyanna on me. Let's hit it."

Ashton Sullivan has been my best friend since I was a little girl. Her family is like my family and after next weekend, we'll be official sisters. Growing up, I loved going to the Sullivan's and absorbing their family vibe. It has always just been me and my mom, and while people assume we're close because of it, that hasn't always been the case. The reality is my mom spent most of her adult life searching, unsuccessfully, for a man. That is, until last year when she met Mike and fell in love. Since then, Mom and I have grown closer, and she's become the mom I had always wanted. Supportive, loving, and present.

Well, as present as she can be no longer living in Lexington. Mom and I talk every day, she calls Ben when she has an idea she can't convince me of, and she and Patty, my future mother-in-law, have become good friends. I suppose the change in my mom is what happens when you accept there are good men and are lucky enough to find one of them to love you.

I should know, I realized the same thing.

"Minnie, I really wish Dakota would have come over. She needs a girls' night." I may be a little tipsy as I shout at Minnie, who is sitting on the cushion next to me on Ashton's very comfortable couch. "Sorry! I'm very loud, aren't I?"

"It's okay; you're the guest of honor and can be as loud as you want." Minnie is such a nice girl. I'm glad Owen got his head out of his ass and told her he loves her. I mean, I'd be friends with her anyway, but now she's one of my best friends and it would have been awkward if he'd screwed that relationship up. See, tipsy. I'd never say this stuff sober.

"I am totally the guest of honor. I think maybe I had too many mimosas at the spa. Shh."

"Your secret's safe with me," Minnie whispers as she takes a long drink from her dirty martini. Those look good. Maybe I should try one. I look at my hand and realize I don't have a cocktail. Ashton told me I needed to hydrate and sober up a little. I have no clue what she has planned, but whatever. I hope there's food because I'm starving.

"Minnie, why didn't Dakota come? Does she not like me? I'm very likeable so that makes me sad."

"Piper, you are totally likeable. In fact, you're lovable. Dakota isn't ready for a party atmosphere. Plus, she missed a lot of time with the girls, and right now all she wants is to hang with them."

"I totally get it. I think she's the coolest, and I'd love to hang out with her more. Plus, she gave me the best gift at my shower. Who even knew there was a gadget to clean baseboards!"

Minnie and I continue to laugh as I hydrate. Ashton has been in the kitchen for an hour and won't tell me what the hell she's doing. Minnie insists it'll be worth the wait, but for crap's sake, I'm starving. And I'm sobering up, which is only going to make me tired. I yawn a few times and Minnie's eyes widen before she hops from the couch and runs to the kitchen. When she returns just a few minutes later, she's holding a margarita and as I take it from her hand and declare she is easily my new bestie, my lifelong bestie comes walking into the room with a huge platter.

"What's this?"

"Well, since this night is all about you and your favorites, I wanted to offer all of your favorite foods. So, while you drink a margarita, a current favorite, which is weird because you're normally a whiskey girl but whatever, I've put this together." Ashton waves her hand across a large platter of food like she's Vanna White. I scoot forward on the couch to look at her display: sushi, nachos, and sliders. I let out a loud squeal because I can eat the hell out of all of this.

"You are a goddess, and I am forever in your debt, Ash." I don't know how much of that Ashton catches because by the time I'm halfway through my declaration I've stuffed a handful of nachos in my mouth.

"This is taking fusion to a whole new level, Ashton." Minnie laughs as she takes one of the small plates on the table and fills it with a slider and a few pieces of sushi.

The girls and I sit and stuff our faces with the amazing food Ashton prepared and finish off another couple of drinks before scrubbing our faces and putting on our pajamas. Yep, party animals. But, this is what I wanted. I wanted my closest friends, good food, and even better drinks on a night where we talk about the men in our lives, share secrets, and watch at least one romantic movie.

Once we've each changed and are ready for bed, we quickly clean up the leftovers—there aren't many—and then snuggle into Jameson and Ashton's big cozy bed. Ashton clicks on the television and ques up my favorite romance movie of all time, *50 First Dates*. This movie makes me laugh, believe in true love, and want to go to Hawaii. Which is where we're going for our honeymoon. I cannot wait. I just hope this PMS or whatever hormonal action I have is gone after the stress of the wedding is behind us.

After a few minutes, Minnie clears her throat and sits up from where she's lying. "Girls, I have a question." Ashton and I both sit up and look at her quizzically. "Do my boobs look bigger? I swear they've grown in the last few weeks. I went in for my final dress fitting last week and the seamstress seemed concerned with how the bust was fitting. Ash did you have the same problem?"

"No, but my dress is a little different, remember? I don't think they look bigger. What'd Owen say? I mean, he'd be the one to notice. That guy can't keep his hands off you; he probably has them memorized."

Minnie flops back down on the pillow and sighs. "He does love my boobs. Well, and my ass. He's really an equal opportunity groper. Damn, I love that guy."

Ashton and I laugh, and although we never really pay attention to the movie, I have the best night with my girl-friends. We stuffed ourselves, we laughed, we cried, and we even compared boob sizes. All in all, a perfect bachelorette party.

Chapter 3

Ben

This is not how I expected to be spending the last few days before our wedding. I'm currently elbows deep in bleach and Lysol. Three days ago, Piper came down with a nasty flu bug, and she's either been nauseous, vomiting, or asleep. Each day she'll have a surge of energy and send out a slew of texts to everyone making sure the wedding is on schedule. Our moms stopped by yesterday and took her phone away from her, hiding it somewhere even I don't know about. My mom said she'd tell me the location tomorrow so I'm able to return it to my bride.

I spent an unordinary amount of time convincing Piper I did not know where the moms had hidden her phone. Once she finally conceded that I too was in the dark, she let out a frightening laugh and said the joke is on the moms as she reached over and grabbed her tablet from the side table. Then, she sent off a message to the gang and told them if anyone rats her out to a mom they are dead to her. I won't lie, I kind of like this side of Piper. She's a little more feisty than usual.

Tomorrow is our rehearsal dinner and while that pre-wedding event is being handled by my parents and is at their house, we have a lot of work to do here before Saturday. I told Piper this is probably why she got sick. She insists it was Ashton's assortment of sushi, nachos, and whatever else junk food they ate last weekend. When her mom tried to explain food poisoning is different than what she's experiencing, she threatened to ban her from the house. Yeah, she may be a little bridezilla right now.

When I woke up this morning exhausted, I had an overwhelming need to clean this entire house—with bleach. I cannot get whatever plague Piper has contracted. With my luck, I'll wake up on our wedding day praying to the porcelain god and look like a zombie in our wedding photos. None of that would fare well for the wedding night. Priorities.

"Son, can you put that bleach down and take off the rubber gloves long enough to come help Landon and me with this arbor?"

"Very funny, Dad. Yeah, I'll be right there."

I remove the gloves and toss them in the sink before taking the time to wash them thoroughly. Bleach may kill germs but it also stinks to high hell. Once I'm done with that, I head outside toward where my dad and Landon are setting up the arbor. When we decided to have the wedding here, I knew the spot we'd exchange our vows. It's the exact location where I fell in love with Piper. Well, that's not true. I fell in love with her every day from the moment I approached her at Country Road and kissed her senseless without even realizing who she was.

Our road to get here wasn't easy, and it wasn't without a little drama, but I wouldn't change a thing. When I first decided to buy this house, I wasn't sure where my life was headed or who I was going to spend it with. Then I encountered a beautiful redhead at the local watering hole, and my entire world turned upside down. Damn, I need to write that down. Piper wanted us to write our own vows, and I've been playing games on my phone instead. Put Piper in front of me and I will tell her four hundred different ways I love her. Put us in front of a crowd and I stutter and say "uh."

I pull out my phone to tap out notes about my vows before I hear tires on the gravel behind me. Turning, I see a delivery truck pulling in. I assume it's the tent, dance floor, and tables for the reception. I tap out the last of my notes on my phone when I hear my name shouted again. This time, instead of my dad, it's Landon. I flip him the bird. Fucker. Obviously, I'm busy.

Satisfied my notes will make sense later, I continue toward my dad and Landon. The ceremony will be staged so Piper and I stand under the arbor with the stream that runs behind our property as a backdrop. That was my only requirement for the wedding. Well . . . and whiskey. Lots of whiskey.

"About time. I thought I was going to have to adopt Landon to thank him for all of his hard work."

"Haha, Pop. I had a thought for my vows and needed

to get them in my phone before I forget."

"Yeah, Mr. Sullivan, Ben has to write his own vows. I have fifty bucks that says he'll cry like a baby."

"Oh Landon, I'm not a sucker. We all know my son is going to lose his shit the minute Piper walks down the aisle. Hell, all those guys are going to lose it when their women walk down the aisle. Myself included. When are you going to find yourself a beautiful woman to spend your life with, Landon?"

I laugh as I lift a piece of the arbor for my dad to hammer. Landon is the last of the four of us who is single. He had a little flirtation going with one of the bartenders at Country Road, but he finally accepted she is spoken for. Of course, it took him actually meeting the girlfriend for him to accept he wasn't in the running for soul mate. Of the four of us, Landon is the one guy I would have expected to already be settled down. Just shows what I know.

"It's not for a lack of trying, that's for sure. I'm in no hurry, sir. My future is out there; I just haven't found her yet."

"Ah, Landon. You've always been such a good guy." I hear the sweetest voice speak, and I smile before turning. I once told Piper she had a voice smooth as honey and I could listen to her read the phone book to me every night. She called my bluff and literally read a page from the phone book each night for a month after she moved in. Somewhere around *Banning*, I threw the book across the room and tackled her until she was screaming my name. We never picked up the phone book again, but her voice is still the sweetest sound of my day.

"Baby, what are you doing? You should be in bed." She looks better, but that doesn't mean anything. She's been going back and forth between looking well and being sicker than a dog.

"Bentley, if I lie in that bed another minute I'm going to go insane. It's bad enough the moms stole my phone. Now, my iPad charger is missing. Y'all have some explaining to do because I can't be without my technology!"

My dad snorts as Landon has the good sense to turn away from Piper before laughing. "Paul, don't mock me. I'm getting married in three days. *Three!* I have been lying in that bed for what feels like half my life! Oh! Oh, my goodness! It's beautiful."

I watch and will remember for the rest of my life, the look on Piper's face as she realizes what we're working on. Her hand flies to her lips, and the tears fall freely as she begins to sob. My dad nods toward Piper, and I turn to my fiancée and pull her to me. She's shaking as she sobs. I move my hands to her head and pull her face toward me while brushing hair from her face. I plant a quick kiss to her lips before she sighs and then gasps.

"No! Oh my God! I haven't brushed my teeth since my nap! I'm such a mess. How can you handle me?"

"You're not a mess. I mean, you kind of are, but I love you just the same," I say with a scrunch of my nose. "I think a shower is in order. What do you say? I'll walk you back to the house? That okay with you guys?" I ask, turning toward my dad and Landon. Both grunt an approval; I don't question it and walk Piper toward the house. Her sobs are gone and she's sniffling a little before stopping to look at me with wide eyes. Her beautiful brown eyes shimmering with excitement.

"I'm starving. Do we have any food?"

"Pipe, let me get you into the shower, then I'll get you some soup and crackers."

"No way. I want food. Like a burger. Oh my gosh or pasta. Do we have any spaghetti stuff? I could throw down a bowl of spaghetti. No! Rosa's! A breakfast burrito. Yes. Oh, with enchilada sauce for dipping. Yes, that's what I want. Most favorite fiancé in the world. Can we make that happen?"

Piper hasn't stopped talking about food the entire walk back to the house and as she opens the screen door to the kitchen, I pull out my phone and tap a message to my sister. She told me she'd be out later today to help work on some of the unfinished projects. I'm sure she'll stop and grab some food for Piper.

"What are you doing? How do you have your phone? You've had it the entire time? Ben!"

"Relax, baby. Come on, it's shower time. Yes, I've had it. But be grateful. Ashton will be here in a bit, and she's bringing you a burrito with extra enchilada sauce. Plus, she's excellent at finding my mom's hiding places. I bet she finds your phone with no problem."

"You really are the best," she says as she walks into our bathroom and quickly begins brushing her teeth before turning toward me and pulling off her shirt. Damn, she's perfect.

"What are you doing?" My voice is instantly gravelly and my shorts are straining as I look at her standing in only a pair of shorts and a lacy pink bra.

"Taking a shower. What are *you* doing?" I don't have an opportunity to respond before Piper has her shorts off and her hand on my zipper.

"Apparently, taking a shower too."

"Damn straight. I feel a lot better but still a little tense. Know any way we can work out my tension?"

I snort as Piper yanks my shorts down before turning and walking into our shower. I'm a lucky bastard to be marrying this woman. I pause before pulling my boxers off and run to lock the door. It'd be just like my sister to walk in our bedroom. I don't need that much bonding in my life—ever. I shed my shoes, socks, and boxers on my walk back to the bathroom and step into the shower behind her. Piper is facing me when I step in, her eyes closed, and her head in the stream of water. The room begins to fill with steam and my skin tingles from the heat radiating off the water.

While Piper continues to soak her hair, I reach over and pump shampoo in my hand. Once I have enough in my hand, I clear my throat to get Piper's attention. A slow smile takes over her face as she lowers her chin and looks me in the eye. I raise a brow and her smile widens as she takes a small step forward so her hair is no longer under the water.

I slowly begin massaging her head, causing the shampoo to lather and Piper to sigh. Her head falls forward a little as my fingers begin working out the knots in her neck. Even without the flu she's been fighting, Piper has been tense. A wedding will do that to you. After a few minutes of massaging, I tug her head back so her hair is barely under the stream of water. Piper closes her eyes and allows me to move her back a little so I can rinse her hair. I mimic the same process with the conditioner. But, as I do, she squeezes shower gel in her hands and begins washing my chest and eventually makes her way down my abs to my very happy and excited dick.

"Piper," my words are part warning and all sexual tension. It's been almost a week since Piper and I have had sex, and I'm worked the fuck up.

"Mmm . . ."

I don't respond to her purr as I finish rinsing her hair and begin washing her body. My hands stop at her nipples, tugging and pulling them. This grants me another longer and more sexual moan from Piper. I continue my work with one hand as the other makes its descent down her hollowed stomach, she has lost a few pounds with all this wedding stress and the flu, but her curves are still there. The soap rinses from her skin and mine as I quickly find the small patch of hair below her navel. I insert one and then two fingers with ease. Piper's breath hitches at the same time I feel my balls lift, my orgasm imminent.

"Babe," I say, but instead of stopping her, I thrust my hips into her hand. I'm going to come in her hand if she doesn't stop. I pull my fingers from her and release her breast as I turn her toward the wall. Piper squeals and takes a step out so her legs are farther apart. Her face is to the side, and I begin kissing her as I bend my knees slightly to line up with her entrance. In one thrust I enter Piper, and she gasps into my mouth as I continue to kiss her.

The feeling is too good and I'm not sure how long I can last, so I reach around and find her little nub. Two quick flicks and Piper's forehead is on the shower wall, her orgasm building. She begins thrusting her hips toward me and that's my undoing. Like a goddamn pubescent teen, I come first and Piper quickly follows. Her breaths are labored, and her head is still resting on the shower wall.

"That was exactly what I needed."

"Me too," I agree while pulling out from her.

"And a burrito. I could totally go for that burrito now."

I laugh and turn Piper toward the water so she can rinse off the evidence of our love making before I do the same. Once we're both clean, we exit the shower and I grab her towel before taking mine from the rack. Once we've toweled off, I walk to our room and pull a pair of jeans from the laundry pile on the chair in the corner.

"When we're married, do you think you'll actually put the clothes away after you fold them?" Piper asks as she puts her bra on.

"Unlikely. I don't see why. Ya know, if it ain't broke . . ."

"Good point. I mean, we've lived in sin this entire time. Why change it now?" she teases.

"Hey," I say, walking toward her now that I'm dressed, "I may not put clothes away after I fold them, but at least I remember to hang my wet towel up. I'm only one man, baby, I can't do it all."

I walk out of the room to Piper laughing and shouting my name.

"Bentley James Sullivan, the towel is still on the floor!"

I laugh all the way into the kitchen where I find my

sister unpacking food and mumbling something about afternoon quickies. Like she's one to talk. I've walked in too many times to her and Jameson's discarded clothes across the living room and sounds from the bedroom a brother should never hear coming from his sister.

I may be getting married in three days, but the day my sister and Jameson finally settle down will be one of the happiest days of my life. My best friend and my sister. I never saw it coming. Apparently, I was the only one. Damn small-town life.

Chapter 4

Piper

I have no idea why the girls are giving me a hard time for wanting to go to bed. At eight o'clock at night. On a Friday. Sure, it's early. Yeah, we're just having dinner. Okay, we've had a little wine and are being sappy while we tell stories about our first loves. Lucky for me, my first love is the man I'm marrying tomorrow. Which, is why I want to go to sleep. The earlier I go to sleep, the earlier I wake up. *On my wedding day!*

Sure, internally there's a marching band celebration taking place. In twenty hours, I will be Mrs. Bentley James Sullivan. All the notebooks and diaries I doodled that name on as a kid will finally become my reality.

"There she is again, in the bride haze."

I toss a carrot at Ashton in response and then bite into another with gusto before responding. "Yes, I'm in a bride haze. I'm also exhausted after waking up every day this week nauseous. Being sick has worn me out."

"You're not kidding. I didn't realize how much anxiety I've had until last night after the rehearsal dinner. J had to carry me in the house from the truck. At least I haven't had a panic attack but I've been exhausted. It's like my brain just shut down. And I'm really glad my dress isn't clingy. I'm so bloated."

Minnie and I exchange a look before laughing. Of course, she's bloated, Ashton has been dipping her cheesy chips in sour cream all night. Stress eating is no joke. I should know. I think if I hadn't caught that bug or gotten food poisoning, whatever the culprit was, my dress would barely fit.

"What about you, Min?" Ashton asks while dipping another chip in her sour cream.

"What about me? I didn't catch whatever Piper did and don't have much anxiety. I am tired from moving and my body feels like I was run over by a Mack truck. And I don't care what you guys say, my boobs are bigger."

We all laugh and decide we should put the food away and begin our nighttime routine. Earlier today, we were all perfectly tweezed, waxed, and bronzed in preparation for the wedding tomorrow. So, tonight we're applying a teeth-whitening serum and some hair wrap process Ashton wants for her hair. I have no clue what it is or what it does, but she saw it on Pinterest and insisted it was a must for her maid-of-honor hair. By the time we're done it should be a respectable hour for me to go to bed.

I'm standing at the sink, applying the last of the foul-tasting product that promises to give me pearly white teeth when Minnie comes in the bathroom holding my ringing phone in her hand. I look at her horrified because I know it's Ben attempting to video chat. My eyes go wide as Minnie smiles and slides the accept button. Brat.

"Hey, groom to be!" I will kill her.

"Oh, hey," I hear Ben say while standing with my mouth wide open because I need this crap to dry and can't touch my tongue to my teeth. In the background, I hear the guys razzing Ben for calling me, but it only makes me smile. If I could smile, but I can't.

"Your blushing bride is just finishing in the bathroom, but I didn't want her to miss your call. Hold on and I'll get her. Tell Owen if he wants to talk to me to call *my* phone," Minnie says while handing me my phone and turning to walk out.

I quickly finish my serum process before accepting my phone from Minnie. "Thanks, Min," I say sarcastically. Instead of responding, she waves her hand in the air and walks away. Really, we're all blessed to have Minnie in our lives and she knows my sarcasm is in jest. Minnie is the kindest person I know plus, she puts up with Owen's bull. Basically, she's a saint.

"Hey, handsome. Whatcha up to?" I ask, sitting on the toilet.

"Did you just sit on the toilet?"

"Uh, yeah?" Ben looks at me quizzically, and I sigh. "I have some crap on my teeth and need to rinse my mouth but want it to kind of work so I need to stay put," I confess.

"Got it. Well, I only have a few minutes to talk myself. The guys and I are going to check all the lights in the tent and along the pathways before we hit the sack. How're you holding up?"

"Me? I'm fine. I'm more worried about your sister. She ate an entire bag of chips."

"So? She always does shit like that." Ben laughs as I watch him move around our kitchen. He's holding the phone in one hand while opening the refrigerator and pulling out a bottle of water with the other.

"No, this was different. It was like she couldn't get enough. And, I'll be honest. I played it off, but it was making me nauseous." I watch as a concern blankets his face. I hate that he's been so worried about me all week. I think planning my own wedding and binging on a buffet of homemade sushi and nachos was not my best idea. Stress is no joke. I attempt to lighten the mood. "Then there was the crying. It about did me in."

"You're still not feeling well? Babe, you should've gone to the doctor. Do you want me to come take you in to the clinic?"

"Oh stop. If you'd seen her eating you'd gag too. It's fine. I feel fine. It's in waves, which means it's probably me getting my period. Sorry about that. No comment about Ashton crying?"

"My sister is a nut, I gave up trying to figure her out. But, if you're sure you're okay, I won't drive over and take you in." I hear the guys yelling for him in the background and know I should let him go.

"I promise, it's only stress. Go do what you need with the lights. If I haven't said it yet, I love you, Bentley Sullivan." The boyish grin I love so much appears and the little butterflies he gives me take over any nausea I may have had. "You are making all of my childhood dreams come true. I can never thank you for making our day so absolutely perfect."

"I love you too, Piper. The day hasn't happened. I could still blow a circuit and the lights not work." He's teasing, but I know the reality is, it's a real possibility. We both laugh and agree maybe his dad should have the backup generator ready just in case.

"I'm going to go and help Minnie and Ash. I'll see you tomorrow." I stand from my perch on the very uncomfortable toilet seat as I prepare to say goodbye, but Ben stops me.

"Hey, Pipe?"

"Yeah?"

"Thank you for making me the luckiest man in the world. You are my dream come true, and I'm grateful you choose me to share your life with."

"Oh, that's the sweetest thing I've ever heard," Minnie sighs from the doorway.

"And the corniest. Say goodbye brother, dear."

I'm no longer alone in my conversation when both Minnie and Ashton appear.

"I guess that's goodnight, Piper. Sleep well ladies, tomorrow we party!" Ben shouts and winks at the screen before it goes black.

I look at my blank screen and wish we'd said no to tradition, and I was at home with Ben. Still looking at the screen, I ask, "Why do we have to sleep apart anyway? That makes no sense. We've been sleeping side by side for months, why should one night matter?"

"Because, sister-to-be, it's how it's done," Ashton responds, pulling my attention from my phone to her, but I don't reply. I can't.

Ashton is standing before me looking like a modern and sassy version of Medusa. Pieces of fabric are tied all through her hair, which make them look like little serpents. My face must give away the amusement because Ashton places one hand on her hip as she pops it out and her other hand is flipping me the middle finger.

"Do not make fun of me, Piper. You may be the bride and my best friend but I will kick your ass. Just you wait, my hair is going to be awesome tomorrow and everyone will be jealous."

"Uh, Ashton, you know we're wearing our hair in low loose fitted buns, right?" Minnie seems equally baffled by this hair situation.

"Yeah, I don't think we discussed you going off the rails with hair. What kind of bridezilla would I be if I didn't demand uniformity?" I laugh but Ashton doesn't. Minnie looks at me quizzically, and I shrug in response.

"What's next, Ashton? A different dress? Are you planning on showing up in white to show up the bride?" I tease because she'd never do anything remotely close to that. But then I see the tears and realize we may have taken our jabs a little too far.

"Oh, Ash, I'm sorry. I didn't mean anything by it." Minnie looks absolutely horrified at the idea of making Ashton cry.

Reaching over to the toilet paper, I unroll a handful

and thrust it toward Ashton. Once she's blown her nose and let out a few huge sobs, she composes herself and looks at me.

"Sorry. I think I'm more stressed about this weekend than I thought. I know the hair is dumb, but I wanted to look pretty on your special day. I love you guys so much. Oh my God! Why am I crying again? It won't stop. This is the worst period ever. If it would just start. Poor J, he's been on pins and needles for weeks."

"Oh hush, you wear your hair however you want, both of you. I don't want this being a thing. I want you comfortable and happy. And, lucky me, I'm going to start too," I sigh. "Poor Ben. This honeymoon is going to be less sexy and more about cramps and chocolate. How about you, Min? Are we synced up?"

"Probably, that would explain these big things," she says pointing to her chest and we nod in agreement. We're all a mess.

By midnight, we're exhausted and I have no doubt I'll fall asleep quickly. Minnie bid us goodnight and headed into the spare room. A few months ago, that was Ashton's room, but it has now been returned to a guest room and Jameson's niece's home away from home. Hope is also our flower girl tomorrow. She's feisty and, essentially, a small version of Ashton. We all love her.

I'm going to sleep with Ashton in her bed. This reminds me of when we were growing up and I spent most weekends at her house. We'd lie in our sleeping bags and tell stories about boys we liked and all the cool clothes we'd eventually buy when we were making our money. As models, obviously. I never told Ashton the boy I crushed on the most was her brother. She says she never knew, but I know that too is a lie. She knew. How could she not? I mean, I practiced signing my name as "Mrs. Bentley Sullivan" daily until high school. Then, I watched from afar as he became the most popular boy in school, dating the most popular girl.

The night he blew back into town and turned my world upside down with a single kiss, I knew my life would never be the same again.

Jameson & Ashton

One week before the wedding day

Chapter 5

Ashton

My brother is a jerk.

My best friend is a pain in the ass.

Okay, neither of those statements are true. Both Ben and Piper are superb human beings, and we are blessed to have them in our lives. Yes, that's much better for my maid of honor speech. A speech. In front of people. Fine, the majority of people who will be at the wedding are family and close friends.

And, I don't *have* to give a speech, I want to give a speech. This is, of course, after I sing at their wedding. Again, in front of people. This is a new thing for me, and because I'm the jerk and pain in the ass, I decided to go balls out and sing and give a speech all on the same day.

Go me!

"Babe, do you know where my clippers are?"

Jameson Strauss. Damn he's a fine-looking man. If

I don't answer him, he'll come find me. Not only will he find me, but he'll be shirtless and sweaty from his workout. I went from being a jerk to a lucky bitch in one thought. I'm also a horny bitch. I haven't been able to get enough. I swear, it reminds me of the weeks we were living together and sleeping together in secret; I'm ready to pounce at the drop of a hat. Not that he's complaining. Hell, no. My guy loves some sexy times and when I'm the one to initiate? He's even more turned on.

"Hey, did you hear me?" Jameson is standing in the door to the dining room where I'm sitting. Papers are strewn across the table in my efforts to write the stupid speech. Plus, the music sheets for the song I'm singing are mixed in with all of this. I really should be a little more organized. The thought of the song has me doing the other thing I've been doing a lot lately—crying.

"Whoa, Ash, what's wrong? Why are you crying?" The concern in his voice makes my tears fall even faster.

"I . . . I . . . don't know!" Yep, I've lost my damn mind.

"Shh, it's okay." Jameson drops to his knees and pulls me toward him. The moment my cheek hits his chest—his warm and sweaty chest—I relax, but the tears don't stop. Seriously, they are like a freaking faucet. Oh, he's so cuddly.

And half naked.

I snuggle into him and sniff the scent that sends my ovaries into overload. My hormones are bouncing around like damn grasshoppers. Granted, he's a little more stinky than usual but for some reason, today, that is enough to do me in. I sniff him again and sigh at the smell that is one hundred percent Jameson Strauss, my favorite smell in the world. I can't believe I deprived myself of him for years.

"Did you just sniff me?"

I nod in response. I need more of him. In me or on me; I need more. Straightening my back, my chest rises and I feel his body stiffen in awareness. My hold on Jameson tightens before I poke the tip of my tongue out and swirl it around his neck. A low groan rumbles from the back of his throat, and I feel how turned on he is.

Who am I to deny such an obvious invitation? I slide my hands back and forth along his back, allowing my nails to scrape his skin. Before I'm able to do much more, he lifts me up and my legs go around his waist as he lays me on top of the table.

"You're playing with fire, baby."

"Mmm . . . burn me, Jameson."

Without another word, Jameson steals my lips with his own, and I melt into the table. My legs are still wrapped around his waist and his lightweight workout shorts do little to restrain his hardening erection. I lift my hips and the brief contact almost creates an orgasm. I'm like a damn firecracker ready to go off.

I don't have time to contemplate my almost orgasm because Jameson is tugging down my tank top to expose by breasts to him. The cool air from the ceiling fan causes my nipples to harden just as he flicks one with his tongue.

Our sex is always phenomenal but something about these spontaneous encounters makes it even more so. Jameson and I have always had an attraction, but the moment we quit lying to ourselves and everyone else and made our relationship official, the phenomenal sex became something much more. We're combustible. Each tug, lick, and thrust is full of passion and heat. Each time we're together, I can't believe it will get better, but each time it does.

When Jameson makes love to me, I feel treasured and loved. When he fucks me like he's about to now, I feel desired and beautiful. I can't wait another minute and begin tugging off the cotton shorts I'm wearing. Clearly impatient, Jameson smacks my hand out of the way and does the honors. I giggle a little, but the look in his eyes instantly turns me from smiling and giggling to the verge of an orgasm from a look. How does he do that?

"Fuck, Ashton, you're so goddamn beautiful."

Smiling, I sit up and wrap my hand around his neck, pulling him toward me. I kiss him with everything I have, hoping he knows how much he means to me. I don't have a chance to deepen the kiss before Jameson slides his hands under my ass and lifts me up as he thrusts into me. It's quick, it's hard, and it's glorious. His hands stay under me, keeping me in place with him as he thrusts into me. Each movement pushes him deeper into me. It only takes seconds before my orgasm peaks. Throwing my head back, I let out a cry that rivals a howling coyote.

Jameson immediately follows me. With his chin to his chest and his eyes clenched, I can tell he's trying to hold on, to ride out his orgasm. He fails and comes with a vengeance.

"Baby, why are you crying?"

Shit, I didn't know I was. "Sorry. I don't know why. I'm not sad. That was fanfuckingtastic. That orgasm started in my toes and made its way to my head like a rocket. Maybe your dick tapped my tear starter or something." I mock and tease because I have no idea why everything is making me cry.

"Doubtful. You'd tell me if something was wrong, right?"

"Of course. I'm sorry," I say as he pulls from me and stands up. His shorts are only around his ankles so he pulls those up while handing me my own. I don't bother putting them on and, instead, start walking toward our room and the shower.

"Hey, don't walk away." Stopping to look at him, I smile. The tears have stopped but I see the concern on his face and realize how much my emotional roller coaster affects him.

"Dude, your jizz is running down my leg. I'm just heading to the shower." When in doubt, go with humor and an eyeroll. "Look," I say, walking toward him. My hand goes to his chest where his heart is beating a mile a minute. "I'm fine. The song, the speech . . . they're giving me some anxiety. Tears are a given when I'm a stressed-out mess. Plus, I'm probably about to get my period so this will all be over in a few days. Don't worry your sexy self. Now, are you going to shower with me or do I have to wash my own back?" I tap his chest with my hand as I dramatically pivot and begin walking, a little extra sway to my hips.

Before I know it, Jameson's rushing toward me, and I'm running from him, laughing. He catches me just as I make it to our bedroom door. His arms wrap around me from behind as he leans down to whisper in my ear.

"If it's too much, don't do the song. They'll understand.

I don't like seeing you stressed. It makes me hurt for you."

And, cue the tears. "You can't say stuff like that," I say, turning toward him. "How is a girl supposed to keep it together when you're sweet? I'll be fine. You'll be there, and I'll just sing to you like I always do. Now, come wash my back."

Jameson growls and smacks my ass when I step into the bathroom. I know the song and the speech are creating anxiety. I know I should probably talk to my brother and Piper. I also know I won't. I'll suck it up and make this day everything they both want and deserve. I can lose my shit another day.

Chapter 6

Jameson

"**M**innie, are you sure you and Owen can handle things next week?" I know the answer. It's a stupid question. Minnie runs my business better than I do. And Owen? Since she came into his life he's a completely different person. He's always been one of my best friends but settling down with her? It's made him more reliable.

"Whoever said there are no stupid questions was a liar. Yes, Jameson, I'm sure. This is a huge thing for Ashton, and I know how special you want to make the week. Go, enjoy. Make her dreams happen."

I flop into my chair dramatically. Some days I have no idea if I'm doing the right thing. I've been tossing around the idea of booking a recording studio for Ashton since she started singing again. I talked to her parents and, although they had reservations at first, both agreed this may be exactly what she needs. But, they haven't seen her over the last few weeks. The idea of singing at the wedding, an event that will only be attended by the people she's closest to, has put stress on her and she is not handling it very well.

Not to mention, I may have talked to her dad about a very important question I plan on asking her. But, seeing as how she's been crying at the drop of a hat for the last month or so, I can't see any of this going well.

"Maybe I should cancel." I should. I need Minnie, who has quickly become one of Ashton's best friends, to tell me to do it.

"You're an idiot. You should not cancel." Minnie looks at me like I've completely lost my mind. "You are going to take your girlfriend, the one you've asked her father for permission to ask a very important question, on a trip where you'll smother her with love and make two of her biggest dreams a reality. Stop being a ninny."

"A ninny? And what two? The studio time is a given. She's wanted to sing a Dolly Parton song and have it on CD since she was a kid. But, what's the other?"

"Marrying you," she scoffs. "Seriously, how do you run this successful business?"

"Umm, Min, you run my business at this point."

"Excellent point. I should give myself a raise."

We both laugh, and the tension I was feeling earlier dissipates. Our days rarely vary, and that's not necessarily a bad thing. In fact, it's a blessing. When I started this company, I had no idea what I was doing. But, over time, Strauss Construction has become quite successful and we've built an excellent reputation. In the past year, I've hired and promoted Owen to foreman and brought Minnie on to run the office. It's freed my time to build community relationships and work toward larger projects, away from the smaller remodels we've been doing.

This past weekend at my lake property with the guys for Ben's bachelor party really solidified that I'm moving my life in the right direction. A year ago, we were all single and not nearly as successful or happy as we are now. What a difference a year makes. Hell, last summer I would have been at my cabin with a different girl every weekend. Sure, I was trying to screw a certain brunette out of my mind and my memories, but regardless, it's how I would have been spending my time.

Instead, the four of us packed up our trucks and headed for a weekend of fishing, whiskey, and razzing the groom-to-be. Ben makes picking on him easy since he is so in touch with his feminine side and has no problem talking about his love for Piper. I, on the other hand, hold back a little. I mean, the woman I love is his little sister. The last thing he wants to hear is about how she prefers reverse cowgirl on any given night. Boundaries and what not.

Monday nights are still guys' night. We meet up at Country Road for the football game, beers, and wings. It's a bonus for me because my girl works there, and I get extra special attention. Except tonight, instead of working as usual, Ashton is with Piper and Minnie, working on last minute wedding stuff. Well, Ash and Minnie are working on stuff. Piper's been sick since her bachelorette party at our house.

I pull up to Country Road and see Taylor's Harley parked under the lights. Taylor's a cool guy and, even though he's technically Ashton's boss, they work side-by-side like equals and share a brother-sister friendship that is like the actual brother-sister relationship Ashton has with Ben. When Ash and I were dancing around each other for years, stupid stubbornness on both our parts, I was a little jealous of how close Taylor and Ashton were. But, now I'm grateful someone is keeping an eye on her when I'm not. Plus it helps to have an ally when I'm trying to pull a surprise trip off and need to get my girl some time off from work.

Country Road isn't a dive bar or the honky-tonk it was twenty years ago. But, it's still a bar, and the idea of my girl working here late at night doesn't always sit well with me. Tonight, it's not rowdy or full of a bunch of people looking to get wasted and hookup. Nope, tonight it's football fans decked out in their favorite team jerseys and over the top accessories, drinking beer and giving each other a hard time.

As I open the door, I'm greeted with a roar of cheers and a few jeers. One of the teams must have scored, and if the level of sound is an indicator, it must be the home team. That'll make Landon happy. I spot the man himself high-fiving a group of guys at the table next to our usual as I approach.

"There you are; we thought you were bailing on us." Owen is already pouring me a pint of beer before he finishes his statement. I lift it to my mouth and instead of responding with words, I flip him off. That about covers it.

"What's the score?"

"The Pack just ran it back to make it ten nothing." Landon is beaming with so much pride, you'd think he actually played for Green Bay.

"Looks like we need another pitcher. Should I put in for a few orders of wings?" I ask but don't bother waiting for an answer. I make my way across the room, acknowledging a few guys I know and high-fiving some of my employees sitting at the bar. I need to talk with Taylor and make sure he is still good with me taking Ashton out of town next week.

"Hey man," I say to a waiting Taylor as I push the now empty pitcher toward him.

"What's up? Another?"

"Yeah, thanks. Oh, and a couple orders of wings and a large basket of fries."

After a few minutes, Taylor returns with a fresh pitcher and four icy pint glasses. "You still okay with Ash having next week off?" I ask as I take the handle of the pitcher in my hand.

"Yeah, it's no problem. I knew these two weeks with the wedding and your trip would be chaotic so I planned ahead. Of course, when she gets back I'm going to need her help. Beth put in her notice today."

"Beth? Really? Where's she going?" Beth's a cool girl, and we're friends. Well, before Ashton and I were together, we hung out a bit. In the biblical sense. But, it was never more than a friends-with-benefits situation. She was a welcome distraction with no strings, and we both kept each other company when necessary. Honestly, if it wasn't for Beth I'm not sure if Ashton and I would have taken the next step. Her open flirtation with me in front of Ash really catapulted our relationship.

"No clue. But, it sucks for me. She's one of our best waitresses."

"Bummer. Hopefully you'll find someone soon. You haven't mentioned next week to Ash, have you? I was still hoping to surprise her after the wedding."

"Not a word. I even put up a fake schedule for next week. She asked why we were doubled up a few days, but I played it off like there was extra inventory and shit to do. She looked relieved. What's up with her lately?"

"I have no idea." I sigh. "She says it's stress. I hope this surprise isn't the catalyst to send her over the edge."

I hang out at the bar, talking to Taylor about the wedding on Saturday. He offered to order the beer and wine we'll have at the reception, so I'm making sure it's still set to be delivered to the house later this week. He may not be one of our childhood friends, but Taylor has been an easy addition to our group even if he hasn't offered much about his past.

By halftime, I've eaten half my weight in wings and fries, had a few beers, and watched Landon dance around like the Packers fan he is. His team takes a twenty-one nothing lead, and I figure I can catch the end of the game at home. I remind Owen of the early start we both have tomorrow before leaving.

One of the upsides to small-town living, other than the low housing prices, is how quickly I'm able to make it across town and home. When I pull up to our house, I park behind Ashton's little green car and sit in the dark for a few minutes. It's hard to believe just a few months ago, Ashton was just my best friend's sister, and the girl I shared two secret encounters with. Now, she's the woman I come home to every night. The woman I hope next week will be wearing a little something on her left hand.

Ashton Sullivan is my future.

Chapter 7

Ashton

Piper Lawrence has been my best friend for as long as I can remember. She's been the one constant in my life, my strongest ally and my biggest supporter. I've never doubted our bond and the depths she'd go for me, and vice versa. Of course, there was that time she was dating my brother behind my back, though. I mean, that shit didn't go over well with me—at all.

Don't get me wrong, it isn't because I don't want them together. If ever there were two people destined for each other, it's those two. It's borderline revolting how cute they are. When I found out, my behavior was less than desirable. Fine, it was childish and selfish. But in my defense, I was in a room with a group of people who knew. They all knew before me. I was hurt. And when I'm hurt or embarrassed, I kind of become a mega asshole.

Except these days. These days, I cry. All the time. And

nap. Goodness a nap is like the greatest thing ever. Except at work. Yeah, falling asleep when you're a bartender is not the best idea. Thankfully, Taylor is the most patient, understanding boss. That man is patient with a capital "P" for putting up with my crying outbursts and lengthy daydreams of napping.

This morning, I woke up and looked at my maid of honor dress and the newly formed spare tire I'm sporting. That sent me into my first fit of tears. Jameson, God bless him, had no idea what to do. As usual. He just held me and consoled me, telling me how amazing I am and how I need to give up singing at the wedding. I won't do it. I worked too damn hard to push through my anxiety about singing for my family and friends. It's still not my favorite thing to do, but I will do it.

I have the perfect song and have been rehearsing for weeks. "When You Say Nothing At All" by Alison Krauss has always been a song I imagined being played at my own wedding. But, as much as I love the song, it really is perfect for Ben and Piper's love story and that makes me happy. Honestly, I don't feel anxious about singing. I don't feel the overwhelming need to vomit nor douse myself in deodorant. Nope, the anxiety seems to be at bay except for the crying. Which makes me tired, and therefore, I nap the day away.

Except today. Today, it's tears, a catnap, and food. I want all the food. Preferably a grilled tuna melt with extra pickles and onion rings with a massive side of thousand island dressing for dipping. Don't judge me; it's amazing. This type of meal is probably why my bridesmaid's dress is fitting a little snugger in the mid-section than I'd like. Thankfully, I invested in the mega version of Spanx and am good to go.

Unfortunately, the amazing dinner I want will have to wait. Tonight is the wedding rehearsal and dinner at my parents' house. Mom is having the meal catered by one of the local Italian restaurants. Carbs are a decent concession to the grilled tuna sandwich.

I'm applying the last of my makeup when I hear Jameson walk in our bedroom. That's not true, I smell him before I hear him. Damn he smells amazing. The citrus body wash he uses mixed with his natural scent and the cologne he spritzed in the other room have my ovaries working overtime.

"You about ready, babe?"

I turn from the mirror to take in my boyfriend. Ladies, Jameson Strauss is by far the hottest piece of man ever to walk the streets of Lexington. He's standing before me in a pair of charcoal gray slacks and a light blue shirt with the sleeves rolled up to his elbows with the collar loosened. The blue and gray tie he has around his neck remains loose and begging for me to tug it, and him, to me. His hair is styled with a little gel in that "I just rolled out of bed looking this sexy" way and his beautiful eyes settle on me appreciatively.

Poof. That was the sound of my panties self-destructing. A small smile appears, and his eyes crinkle at the side like they do when he's ready to pounce me. I know he's thinking of bending me over this sink. The sexual tension in this small space is not only obvious by the look in his eyes, but it's the little tells he has. When Jameson is think-ing kinky thoughts, his breathing speeds up a little, the rise of his chest is more evident. His pupils dilate more when he thinks of bending me over or taking me against a wall. But it's the way a small vein in his neck pulses that always gives away his thoughts. Dirty thoughts.

As much as my libido, and my lady parts, would love to give him what he wants, if we're late, my mom and Piper will kill us. And more unfortunate is the fact that I'm stay-ing at Piper's tonight after the rehearsal to help with all the last-minute wedding crafty crap she insists needs to be done. Okay, it's not crap and had she not been sick all week, we would have it all done and I'd be living out some fantasies with my man.

Pulling myself from my own dirty thoughts, I final-ly respond to Jameson. "Just about. I need to throw a few things in my bag for tonight, then I'm good to go. Oh, and a pillow."

Jameson doesn't respond immediately so I saunter to-ward him, a little more sway in my hips than usual. With my makeup bag in one hand, I slowly walk my fingers up his arm. He shivers. I giggle.

"Put your dirty thoughts on hold, big boy. We're in the home stretch, only two more nights of this pre-wedding chaos. At about this time on Saturday, we'll be partying it up with everyone. And, if we're lucky, tequila will finally appeal to me, and I'll get tequila frisky."

I barely finish my sentence before Jameson is scooping me up into his arms, the hem of my dress lifting to expose my thong, and the hand more interested in the hair at the nape of his neck than holding my makeup bag, drops it to the counter. My laughter intensifies as he grabs a handful of my ass. But the moment he kisses me, the laughter turns to a moan and like every other time he kisses me with such desire. Before I'm able to suggest we could be a few minutes late, Jameson slows the kiss and places a quick peck on my lips.

"You look beautiful, Ashton. I'm a lucky bastard." I roll my eyes dramatically.

"No shit I look good. That's a given," I tease. "You better put me down, those five pounds I've put on with this wedding stress are going to break your back."

"Shut up. You look perfect. And your tits look delectable." His voice is husky and his eyes full of want. Just a few minutes . . .

"Nope, put me down, big guy. Piper will kill us both. I love you and would love nothing more than to allow you an opportunity to feast on my tits, and anything else you'd like, but we've gotta go. Shit, we have twelve minutes to get there." I squirm from his hold and rush to my bag, tossing in my makeup bag.

"Relax, Ash. It's three miles from here. We'll be fine. Get your shit, and I'll lock the house."

I nod in response as I grab Jameson's T-shirt he tossed on the bed earlier. If I'm not sleeping with him tonight, I'll at least be comforted by his scent and clothes. I walk out of the room and toward the front door and see him standing waiting for me. I will never understand how I deprived myself of this for so long.

Owen & Minnie

One week before the wedding

Chapter 8

Minnie

"Ari, please put that down." My four-year-old niece is pushing every one of my buttons today. I love her like she was my own and as much as she wants to help me pack my belongings, she's creating more work for me than anything else. Not that I have a ton of things to pack. When I moved into my sister's house a few months ago to help care for her kids while she worked on her sobriety and began grieving the loss of her husband, I brought the bare minimum with me, leaving my former life in the dust.

Now, moving in with my boyfriend to his newly purchased house, I realize how little I have. Clothes, a few pictures, my laptop, and my bedding is about it. Owen isn't in much better shape himself. He's been in an apartment with his roommate and best friend, Landon, for years. By now, they've taken to a lottery on who gets what furniture. Since both guys recently purchased homes and are moving out, they wrote out the names of items on scraps of paper and put them in a hat. Each took turns drawing from the hat to determine what furniture and major kitchen or electronic item they took.

So, we're starting our life together with a massive television, a blender, Owen's bed, the kitchen table, and my bedding. I wanted to put this move off another week to allow us time to shop for furniture and the basics but Owen wouldn't wait. He hates staying here at my sister's house, says he feels like she still doesn't trust him and is judging him. I hate staying at his place because . . . well, I'm not quiet in bed and feel like Landon is in the room with us.

"Sorry, auntie . . ." I hear her sniffles before I realize what Arizona has said. Turning toward her, I see she's broken a little ceramic turtle I had on my dresser. I smile at her because it holds no real significance, and I know she feels awful.

"Ah, chickadee. It's fine. You're being a big help to me. What do you say we put this packing off until later and go have a popsicle on the deck?"

"Okay." She sniffles again. I hate that she feels bad so I pull her into a hug and tickle her sides until the sniffles turn to giggles.

"Is Uncle Owen coming over for popsicles?"

Be still my heart. Arizona just started calling Owen her uncle a few days ago. It's like she knows it drives my sister nuts and insists on proving a point. Owen and Arizona have always had a connection and bonded quickly over his love of using an excessive amount of ketchup. He talked to her like a person and not a child with no opinions. She loved that and ultimately, him. Dakota is still warming up to him but knows how much better for me he is than my ex, Kent. Kent was a dick of epic proportions. But if it wasn't for him and his lack of empathy, I wouldn't have moved to Lexington and never would have met Owen.

Speak of the devil. Ari and I are sitting on the steps of the deck with our popsicles—cherry for me and grape for her—when he walks up behind us.

"What's up ladies? Oh cherry, let me get in on that." Owen tugs my hand toward his mouth as he sits down next to me. The mischief in his eyes has me giddy and wishing little ears and eyes weren't nearby. He takes the popsicle in his mouth, his tongue swirling before he sucks the dripping juice. I sigh. He laughs. Fucker.

"Uncle O, we can get you your own. You wanna grape like me? It's the best!"

"Nah, squirt. I'll share your auntie's. How was your day? Did you get packed?" I give up "sharing" with him and hand him my treat as I recount my packing efforts and the realization neither of us have much to move in and, once again, maybe we should wait.

"Negative. Not happening. We're moving in tonight. I already have my stuff there, and the bed is ready to go. That's all we need until next week. I told you, we'll drive to that damn store you went on and on about and buy everything we need."

"Ikea, babe. It's Ikea. I know. Do you think this is smart? We've only been together a few months. What if you hate living with me? What if you hate that I have seven boxes of tissue all over the place? What if you realize I'm a moody . . ." I pause and look at Ari who has moved away from us and is bent over trying to not get the dripping juice from her popsicle on her clothes. She's unsuccessful. "Asshole," I whisper.

"Minnesota." I love when he says my full name. Only him.

"Owen."

"Look, I know it's fast, but when you know, you know. I wasted too much time trying to figure my shit out and now that I have, I'm done screwing around. You and me. That's what it's about. And you can have five hundred box-es of tissue. Hell, put one on every surface in the house. I. Do. Not. Care. I care about you. I love *you*."

Damn him. He spent months having me wondering where I stood in his life and now that he's admitted his feelings it's like he can't stop declaring them. Each time I fall a little more in love. Owen Butler is the swooniest of boyfriends ever. He surpassed any book boyfriend I had the day he told me he loved me, and now, he just solidified it.

"'Cept me, right Uncle O? You love me and Cali too. We're your best girls."

Arizona is staring at Owen with a look that shows she means business. I know, and Owen knows, she has him wrapped around her little finger. He picks her up and places her in his lap, sticky hands and ruined outfit and all, before leaning over and kissing me. It's not full of pas-sion, it's completely appropriate for little eyes, but it is full of promises.

"I love all my girls. I'm very lucky to have you all in my life." Owen pauses as we both hear the slider door. "Even your mommy, Ari." I snicker at his statement. Dakota is one of the reasons Owen and I are together now. She knew how I was feeling, she put in to words what I was struggling to say and set him straight. That doesn't mean she isn't a little leery of how quickly we're moving, but she's supportive because she knows he truly loves me and wants to make me happy. I rest my head on his shoulder as he continues, "I'd do just about anything for you all. But, your auntie, she's my number one. She's the brightest star in my sky."

And, that is why Owen Butler is getting lucky as soon as I can get him out of here. I hear a faint sigh behind me and know that, as much as my sister wants to play tough, she knows why I'm moving out of her house and into Owen's only weeks after making our relationship official. She's been through a lot, and while she still has a long way to go, it's time for all of us. The girls need their mom to be their mom and their aunt to get back to her life.

Chapter 9

Owen

I've been downplaying the size of Minnie's boobs since she started asking me a few weeks ago. When she first asked me if they were bigger I was half listening and said no. If I remember anything from when my parents were together, it's when your woman asks you if anything on her looks bigger or fatter the answer is: "You look beautiful." Always.

At first, that response worked. Then after a few more days she insisted I feel them. Compare them to what they were the week before. Who am I to deny my girl what she wishes? I felt them, all right. And then I stripped her naked and blew her mind on the counter of my new house.

Our new house.

Sure, it's only in my name for now, but it's our home. Well, it's a house with a bed in it. We really do have to go to that Ikea place she keeps talking about. I looked it up online. Seems like a lot of work for me when we make the purchases. If there's a diagram, it means work.

Today, she's standing in the bathroom in only a bra, turning from side to side. I'm watching her poke at her stomach. Her flat and perfect stomach. I snort as she stands board straight and thrusts her chest out. It's bigger, sure. But not in any way I'll ever complain about. What can I say, I'm a tit man?

"Do not mock me, Owen Butler. This isn't funny. I've gotten fat. I've put on the freshman fifteen or something."

I walk behind Minnie, wrapping my arms around her waist and resting my chin on her shoulder. We're facing the mirror and I place a chaste kiss to her shoulder drawing a sigh from her lips. My hands glide across her ribs and up to her voluptuous chest, cupping her amazing tits in my hands.

"You are perfect in every way, Minnesota." She rests her head back on my shoulder and sighs again. A small smile greets me in the mirror, and I kiss her again but this time I give her a little love bite.

"Owen, you have to say that. You want in my pants."

I laugh and let her out of my embrace before smacking her ass. "I get in your pants, or up your skirt, whenever I want. You can't deny this, baby," I tease shaking my ass as I walk away. I hate that she doubts how beautiful she is.

"Did you get a talking to from Jameson like I did?" I ask as I buckle my belt. Minnie walks out of the bathroom and, much to my chagrin, pulls a top over her head, covering herself.

"Yes. Seriously, you'd think he forgot how much time

he spent this past summer out of the office. I think he's nervous Ashton isn't going to appreciate his surprise."

"Oh, she'll appreciate it. Eventually. I doubt right away, though. Knowing Ash, she'll freak out and get mad at him. Then he'll say something chick-like, and she'll melt like she always does. They're nothing if not predictable."

Minnie playfully slaps me on the arm as she walks by and I act injured. She doesn't stop and keeps walking out of the room. Normally, we ride to work together, me dropping her at the office before heading to a job site, but today we won't be driving in together. Tonight, she's going to hang out with her sister and nieces. Since I'll be alone, I decided to head out to Landon's place to hang out. As much as I love living with Minnie and wouldn't change a thing, Landon and I have been roommates for years. It's kind of weird not hanging out.

I follow Minnie to the kitchen and watch as she pulls both of our travel mugs from the bare cupboards. Thankfully most of this week is packed with pre-wedding activities before Ben and Piper's wedding this coming Saturday, and we don't need more than the coffee cups in our cupboards.

Minnie hands me my cup with coffee made exactly how I like it. I'm a lucky bastard, that's for sure. I almost screwed up by letting her go, so lost in my own head and living my life based on assumptions and misunderstandings. The night she agreed to give me a second chance was the best night of my life. That wasn't too long ago either. And, while I know most of our family and friends are looking at us like we're moving too fast, I have no doubt

Minnie is it for me. I told her the other day, it's as simple as the saying "when you know, you know". That's never been truer. Honestly, I knew the minute this beautiful blonde beauty ran into me in the parking lot at work that she was a game changer.

Okay, I didn't know she'd be the woman to make me suddenly believe in love and commitment, but I did know she would be worth getting to know. That is, after I assumed she was there for Jameson. Thank goodness that wasn't the case.

"Do you really think Ashton will be angry, Owen?" Minnie asks as we lock up the house and head for our cars. "I mean, he went to a lot of trouble for this trip and what he has planned."

I open Minnie's door and wait for her to settle in and buckle her seat belt before I kneel before her. "Min, I know Ashton. She's a fight first, ask questions later kind of girl. But the minute she lets it settle in, she'll realize the secrecy and surprise is coming from a good place."

Minnie smiles that beautiful smile of hers, blue eyes dancing, with a glimmer of a tears. My girl is a romantic through and through. "But, babe," I say, standing as she looks up at me and nods, "don't tell her you knew for weeks. She'll be angrier with you than J; it's how she rolls."

"Got it," Minnie says with determination. "See you this afternoon?"

"Yep, I don't think I need to go in the office, I'll just get the stuff from the shop and head to the job site," I reply before leaning down and giving her a quick goodbye kiss.

After sending Minnie off, I walk to my Jeep and hop

in. The weather is starting to change, the days are shorter and the temps cooling so my top is on. While I let my car warm up, I shoot a text off to my crew reminding them of what needs to be done and that I'll be at the site late. Jameson trusting me to run his crew and his business in his absence has been an honor, and I'll be damned if I'm going to let these guys screw off. That's why I told them I'd only be fifteen minutes late instead of the hour it'll probably take me.

My relaxed and carefree morning took two shits before lunchtime. First, the inspector chose today of all days to show up at the site. We're on schedule, and my crew does a good job, but it's still a pain in the ass to stop what I'm doing and deal with that. Thankfully it went well but not before we lost two hours of work. Then, one of the guys on the crew missed the fucking safety lecture I gave him and wasn't wearing his safety glasses. Not to worry, he has both eyes, but he did have to run to the clinic to make sure he didn't scratch it or anything more damaging.

I text Minnie and let her know I'm not going to make it for lunch. She's the best girlfriend on the planet and had a sandwich delivered to the site for me. I send her a text thanking her, and she tells me she's worried I'll skip lunch altogether. See? Lucky bastard. Also, I'm known for being a little angry when I'm hungry or "hangry." I think part of her forethought is my crew.

I'm thinking how lucky I am when I knock twice on

Landon's shop door. He looks up at me from where he's sanding and rolls his eyes. "Dude, seriously. Did you just get a hummer in the car or something?"

"Fuck off man. Don't talk about Minnie like that," I warn.

"Minnie wouldn't care, she loves me. Tell me what's got you with that pussy grin on your face."

"Dude, what's your problem? Hummer and pussy grin? That doesn't sound like you. You're the nice one of our group."

"Nah, man. That's Ben. I'm the quiet one. The thinker. Ya know what I'm thinking? I'm fucking sick of being the last one single. I'm watching all you guys find women, and I'm over here at Sunday dinner with my parents having my mom attempting to set me up with every single girl at church. It's pathetic."

Landon's always been the logical one in our group, the assessor. He's a thinker and observer, never one to do anything in life without carefully weighing the options. I've always depended on him to point out when any of us are about to do something stupid.

Landon is precise, meticulous. Even though he looks at most things in life with a logical approach, his true talents lie in turning abandoned wood into beautiful art. He's currently finishing up his wedding gift for Ben and Piper. Keeping the details to himself, he's only told them the size dimensions and weight for hanging purposes. Curiosity has been killing Piper the last few months as she stares at the designated blank wall in her house, waiting for the gift to arrive.

So as much as I'm used to my confident, meticulously assessing best friend, this version on Landon? Defeated and down on himself? That's not my best friend. Landon Montgomery is happy. He's almost fucking *jovial*.

"Man, you need to get laid. This sad panda shit is weird."

"Sad panda? What the fuck, Owen? Who talks like that?"

"Minnie. Don't ask. Anyway, stop looking. That's what I'd say. None of us were looking for love, and it smacked us in the face. Some of us literally. It'll happen. Hell, don't they say weddings are a great place to meet women? This may be your lucky weekend."

"Kill me now. I know everyone at this wedding. You've got to be kidding me. I'll probably be seated at the kiddie table as it is. Ignore me. My mom told me there's another "lovely young lady" coming to dinner Sunday. I thought when I bought this place and moved out she'd back off. I was wrong. So very wrong."

I laugh with Landon and start helping him. I'm the only one who has seen this project. At first, it was a simple piece of abandoned barn wood. It's not what the piece is that makes it beautiful, it's an abstract, so to me the beauty is more in the way he's crafting, sanding, and finishing the wood. It's what they feature in fancy magazines you only see in doctor's offices or on television. We've tried to get him to sell his work, but he refuses. So now we wait for a special occasion and hope he gifts us something.

Hours after I arrived and one large pizza later, we call it a night and I head home. The sky is scattered with stars and a bright moon. Each time I see the moon, I think of Minnie and how much she enjoys sitting in the dark by moonlight. She believes only good things happen under the moonlight, and it's one of the reasons I bought a house with huge windows and a large back deck. My first stop after this wedding business is to buy a double chaise for the deck. I want to hold Minnie in my arms as she lies under the moonlight, happy.

I pull up to the house and smile. Her car is in the drive, the porch light is on, and the rest of the house is dark. It's late, and I know she's in bed so I'm quiet as I open and close the front door. Setting my keys and wallet on the counter in the kitchen, I see a note from Minnie telling me she couldn't wait up but there's water in the fridge. I open the fridge and see not only water but a six-pack of beer, two bottles of wine, fruit, cheese, and bread. I laugh. The necessities.

I'm still smiling after my shower as I climb into bed behind Minnie. Wrapping my arms around her, I snuggle my chin into the spot just above her shoulder. Minnie stirs a little before I hear her sigh, and I close my eyes.

Chapter 10

Minnie

Dakota is the only one I can trust to be honest with me at this point. Although, as my older sister, she's known to be a little brutal when it comes to honesty. When I was ten and asked her if my boobs would ever grow, she looked at me straight in the eye and deadpanned a simple "No." I cried for a week.

Then, the time I was excited to go to my first high school party, she flat out told me I looked like I was heading to a re-enactment of the civil war with my long skirt and blouse. I thought I looked retro. Shows what I knew about fashion at fifteen.

"Dakota, just say it. I'm fat."

"Minnesota, you are not fat. You should stop saying that. I'd prefer my daughters didn't start thinking looks and weight, which it should be noted, neither are an issue for you, are important in life." She has a point.

"You're right. I just don't know what's happening," I whine. I wish I was "wining" with a glass of Chardonnay instead. But, alas, I am not. I have two bottles at home in the fridge. Last night I was tired of not having snacks and drinks in the house so I stopped by the store for necessities: cheese, wine, beer, and water. I also picked up some deli meat, but I ate that in the car on the way home. I'm a mess.

"Min, I hate to break it to you but . . . wait for it . . . you're happy."

"Being happy makes it so I can't wear my favorite blouse because my boobs are popping the buttons? That's ridiculous."

Dakota laughs at me and slides a glass of sparkling water my way. I've noticed my sister is laughing more and that makes me unbelievably happy. Earlier this year, she was in a horrific car accident that claimed the life of her husband. Grief is a bitch and sent her spiraling in ways we never expected. I also didn't expect her needs to completely turn my life around. All for the better but not without first testing everything I thought to be true. Like the strong and determined woman she is, Dakota took the initiative to face her issues and sought treatment. That's what brought us to Lexington, her need to start fresh as Dakota Jennings and not the widow of Jeff Jennings.

"Stop laughing, it's rude." I attempt to pout, but it's for naught as she smirks back at me. Damn her.

"Oh, sissy. I'm not laughing *at* you. Okay, maybe I am since you're looking at me like you want to throw that water in my face. But, it's happy weight. You're in love and instead of going to the gym or working your life away, you're spending it with your friends, family, and your new boyfriend. It's a good thing, Min."

Interesting. I was with Kent for years and never put on any weight. Come to think of it, in comparison I was never blissfully happy. Owen makes me happy. What's more than happy? That's me. In love and feeling loved.

"I guess. I'm going to need to put the bliss on hold and drop about ten pounds or buy new bras and shirts."

Dakota laughs again before Arizona and Cali appear in the kitchen where we're sitting. Already in their pajamas, I see the tell-tale sign of bedtime on both of their faces. Cali even stops her crawl mid-stride and yawns.

"Auntie, will you tuck me in?"

The girls and I have an even tighter bond after the months I lived here, taking care of them. I know it's hard for Dakota to see me caring for her girls sometimes so I shoot her a quick glance, and she's shaking a bottle for Cali.

"Go ahead, I'm going to give this one some meds before her bottle. I think she's cutting another tooth."

I nod and scoop Ari into my arms, causing her to giggle. Once we're in her room, I place her on the ladder to her bed. My dad and brother put together a bunkbed that also acts as a castle. Nothing but the best for the princess of the family.

"You all cozy, chickadee?" I ask, standing on a foot stool which allows me to peer into her bed.

"Yep," she says, popping her "p." "Momma said you and Uncle O get to dress fancy this weekend. Will you come here to show us?"

"We can't, baby. Remember our friends, Ben and Piper?" I ask, and she nods in response. "They're getting married and we have to be there early to help them. But I'll make sure to send your momma pictures. Will that be okay?"

Ari yawns and offers me a slight nod before turning to her side. I guess this conversation is over. I snicker and place a kiss to the top of her head and walk out of the room, turning the light off. I pad my way down the hall back to the kitchen where Dakota is sitting alone. I assume she put Cali in her bed. The girls are sharing a room for now but when Cali is teething, she's a fussy sleeper. If Dakota wants any rest tonight she'll need Cali to sleep in her bed where she is able to comfort her.

"Thanks for that," she says as I sit down.

"Of course. Are you okay?" Gone is the laughing sister from twenty minutes ago. This is how it happens, though. Dakota will have sad days and happy days. Sometimes the sadness and the loss of her husband hits her out of the blue. I think this is one of those times.

"I'm okay. It is what it is. I wish I could figure out what triggers me. I suppose, it's like my counselor says. *Life.*" Dakota sniggers and I smile. "Life is my trigger. How convenient is that?"

"I think it's wonderful. That means you're living, Dakota. It's a good thing. How about this? I need to get . . . scratch that. I *want* to get more active. How about if you and I find a yoga studio or some sort of dance class. We used to love to dance. It'll be good for both of us. Plus, what is it *Elle Woods* said? Endorphins make you happy or something like that?"

"Deal," she says through a yawn.

"And on that note, I'm out of here. I have a furniture-less house to go home to."

"Yeah, you need to handle that. You know Ikea has delivery."

"Trust me, I've contemplated one-clicking the heck out of that site. But, I want to do this with Owen." I hesitate before continuing. "I never did thank you, ya know."

We stand and I find my shoes near the front door. Sliding them on before picking up my purse, I wait for Dakota to respond. She opens the front door and smiles. "You're welcome. He just needed a kick in the ass. I'm always happy to do that. Plus, he's grown on me. I'm happy you've found someone to love you, Minnesota. You deserve it. Appreciate it every single day. Never ever take it or him for granted." Her statement is as much a warning as it is her reminding herself. Dakota and Jeff had an amazing relationship. She was loved and loved him back. I'm happy to have found the same with Owen.

We hug goodnight and as I pull my car out of her driveway, I realize how lucky we are to have my sister in our lives. She's a blessing, and I only hope she finds her new happiness.

The drive to our house is quick, and I only make it through two songs before I'm pulling into my spot next to Owen's Jeep. I see the lights on in the living room and before I get to the front door I hear him yelling at the television. Sports Center. He's very interactive with his programs.

"Come on, man. That was totally out of bounds!" I laugh as I set my purse down on the floor near the front door and kick off my shoes. I walk into the living room to find Owen sitting on a bean bag chair. That's new.

"Hey," I say as he turns his attention from the television to me. Damn that smile.

"Hey, baby. I got bean bag chairs."

"I see," I reply, walking toward him and eying the empty chair, or whatever you call it, next to him. I decide instead of taking up the space on the empty chair, to use his lap instead by straddling him. My movement causes my skirt to hike up exposing my long legs. At least the weight I've put on has stayed in my chest and not made its way to my legs.

"Oh, I like your chosen seat better than using that thing," he flirts, placing his hands on my ass while waggling his eyebrows.

My hands glide up his biceps to his shoulders and eventually behind his neck. I run my fingers through the hair at the base of his neck as I lean forward and kiss him. Owen loves when I'm the aggressor in any activity, specifically those of the sexual nature. Our kiss is sweet and tender at first, but then Owen takes one hand from my ass and places it in my hair and tugs me to him, increasing the intensity of our kiss. This movement sends tingles down my spine and directly to my happy place. The one that I am mindlessly gyrating on Owen's lap. A growl from him has me melting into him. The kiss seems to go on forever as we make-out like a pair of teenagers. Dry humping and gasping as I feel an orgasm building.

I don't have time to think about suggesting we move to the bed because Owen is tugging my panties to the side and thrusting a finger inside me. My head flies back, breaking our kiss as he flicks my clit once then twice before my orgasm crashes into me. Damn that was fast, but it's not nearly enough. I lift myself enough to tug his gym shorts down. Thank the heavens, he's going commando tonight. While I'm tugging his shorts down, Owen holds my panties to the side. I make quick time of lowering myself back down onto him. He fills me to the brim; the man who makes me smile, laugh, and come like a goddamn volcano, nibbles at my neck, and I melt into him.

Owen pulls me forward and captures my mouth with his. Try as I might to control this moment, I fail. Owen sets the pace. Lifting his hips, pulling me to him, again and again. I feel an orgasm building. Dear Lord, I can't get enough of him. I'm so close and can feel by his breathing and his telltale moan he is, too. Then, he shifts his hips as he tightens his grip on my hips, and I explode.

As seconds tick by, I'm able to catch my breath as he kisses my lips gently and pushes the hair that's fallen in my face back. "You okay there, baby?"

I snicker in response and smile. "That was a new move."

"Nah, I've just been waiting for us to have these fancy chairs."

We both laugh until my sides hurt and I lift off him. "I think I need a shower."

"Me too; let's go. We both have a busy few days, we need to get some sleep."

I agree and make my way into the bathroom first. Once he's closed the house he joins me. More kissing, more tugging, more satisfaction. It's the dirtiest shower I've ever taken, and I love every single minute of it.

This is what I've always wanted. To be wanted and adored. For a man to look at me like I've hung the moon and set his soul on fire. Owen does that. He is my lobster. My north star. My soul mate.

The ungodly number of orgasms doesn't hurt either. He's a giver.

Chapter 11

Owen

Ben and Piper are my first friends to get married. I mean, there was Johnny Appleton from high school. Yes, we called him Appleseed. Nobody ever said we were always nice guys. Johnny married the girl he met on spring break during an impromptu trip to Vegas. That marriage lasted long enough for three kids, a mortgage, and a poor decision. By decision I mean, he cheated. Publicly. At The Road. Dumbass.

I didn't go to Johnny's wedding for obvious reasons. Well, mostly because I wasn't invited, but that's not the point. The point is, this wedding, Ben and Piper—or "Biper" as Ashton keeps referring to them—this is the first real wedding I've been to or been in. How we've all made it to thirty and never been to a wedding, I'll never understand.

I thought weddings were like they are on television.

Some overly organized woman with a clipboard and a headset telling us all where to go and what to do. Nope. That isn't how this is going at all. Actually, Ben's ex-girlfriend, Laurel, is taking the role of organizer and mostly because nobody is crazy enough to tell her no. I guess we should all be surprised to see Laurel here but we're not. She was there when Ben declared his love to Piper so at this point, none of this is surprising. Laurel and Piper became friends shortly thereafter, and when Piper needed someone neutral to boss us all around, she immediately thought of Laurel.

Tonight, we're rehearsing the ceremony. I'm not quite sure why we need to do this and none of the guys seem to have an answer. I mean, Piper told me our job was simple—get Ben to the altar, don't get too drunk, and smile for pictures.

Done.

But now, Laurel is standing here talking about posture, pace, and where to put our hands when we're standing. I *want* to put my hands on Minnie's tits as I watch her walk down the fake aisle in the Sullivans' backyard. I don't think that's where Laurel meant for me to put them, so I'm refraining. It sucks because they look amazing in the dress she's wearing. Minnie, not Laurel. My eyes are only on Minnie as she walks toward me and veers to her left. I wink at her and enjoy the blush that lights up her face. Damn I'm a lucky guy.

"Stop eye fucking her, man," Landon teases from my left. Dick.

"Don't be jealous," I tease before we're hushed and

side-eyed by the drill sergeant, aka Laurel.

The rest of the rehearsal goes by quickly. Ben cries, Piper giggles, Ashton fidgets, and my girl smiles at me like she can't wait to speed through this night and get naked. Too bad we still have to get through the dinner, make a toast—yeah, me make a toast—and socialize with our parents.

Yep, Ben and Piper invited all our parents and siblings if there are any. Piper wanted this to be all family and friends, peace and love, or whatever. Since she considers our group to be her family, our actual families are an extension of that. My dad and his girlfriend, Barbara, are here. Minnie's family declined the invitation but were kind enough to send a gift for us to bring in their place.

Tonight, Landon and I will give toasts along with Minnie. Tomorrow at the wedding, the best man, Jameson, and the maid of honor, Ashton, will do the honors. Minnie has been efficient and planned ahead by writing out her speech. I didn't. I figured I'd wing it. I've known both Ben and Piper most of my life. Ben is like a brother to me, and Piper like a little sister. I figure a few stories about each of them to make everyone laugh and causing them to flip me off is perfect.

But after a few beers, a shot, and listening to Minnie give her speech, I don't think I can be a smart ass. I mean, I'll be a smart ass because that's who I am, but I'm not sure the flipping off is in me anymore. Dammit. I had a plan.

Standing and lifting my beer, I take a swig before clearing my throat. I scan the room and see the happiness that surrounds my friends. Their love is obvious not only in how they look at one another but how the group they've gathered looks at them. Each person is not only happy for them as a couple but for who they are individually. That's something to be appreciated.

Minnie gives a sweet and kind speech. She talks about love, happiness, and finding your soul mate. My heart grows a thousand times listening to her. And, yes, so does my dick. I'm not immune, even at a wedding rehearsal dinner. But regardless of what a dog I am, my girl has a way with words. Her kindness, belief in love, and her sweet heart are evident in every word she speaks. When it's my turn I pause. What the hell do I know about relationships? I'm going to kill Piper for making me do this.

"Well," I begin, "that's a tough act to follow. Thanks, babe." The group laughs and Minnie winks at me. "I didn't write any notes or give much thought to what I was going to say. I mean, I know everyone in this room, so this can't come as much of a surprise." The grumbles from the audience confirm my statement. "I did plan on telling an embarrassing story about each of these two. I figured, if they're going to make me wear that suit tomorrow, the least I can do is make them a little uncomfortable." A few people snicker, and my nerves lessen. "But then I sat here watching them. Watching all of you and I realized something, they're doing a fine job of embarrassing themselves." I'm greeted with a few chuckles but they tell me nobody knows where I'm going with this speech. Neither do I but I continue.

"What I mean is, these two cannot keep their eyes or hands off each other. It makes the rest of us feel a little uncomfortable, you guys. Save some of it for the honeymoon." That gets me more laughs and a napkin to the face from Piper. I wink at her before saying more. "Pipe, I've known you for most of my life. You were a royal pain when we were kids. The way you chased after this guy," I say, pointing my beer toward Ben, "was embarrassing. I mean, have you no dignity?"

"Nope. None whatsoever!" Piper shouts, and the room erupts in laughter.

"And you, Bentley James Sullivan. What the fuck took you so long? Sorry for swearing ladies, but Patty," I say, looking Ben's mom directly in the eye, "what's with your son?"

Patty shrugs but sends a sympathetic look to Laurel, who is laughing and shrugging her shoulders in equal confusion. It's all in good fun, and they know it. We all do. Yeah, Ben spent years with Laurel when he left for college and the years that followed. But, his heart and his life are with Piper. That was evident the first night he kissed her at the bar without realizing who she was.

"Y'all know I'm teasing. I love you guys and nothing has made all of us happier than watching you find your way to one another. Your love is evident in everything you say and each word you speak. I, for one, hope I give my lady a smidgen of what you give each other. May your days be filled with laughter, your nights filled with passion, and your lives be forever in love. To Ben and Piper!" I raise my beer in toast as everyone clanks glasses and Piper mouths "thank you" and I catch Minnie looking at me through glistening eyes.

I hold Minnie's gaze for a split second before we both mouth the most important words I'll ever speak to her, "I love you."

Landon

One week before the wedding

Chapter 12

Landon

Another dinner means another set up. My mother is relentless. Of course, I appreciate her efforts. Okay, that's not true. I don't *appreciate* them, I tolerate them. My mother decided four years ago I was wasting time when I should be courting the woman who would call her "mom" and give her grandchildren. I have explained that courting is now referred to as dating, which I do, and there's no timetable for having children. Hugh Hefner anyone? My mom was less than thrilled with that comparison.

She also does not appreciate when I point out she already has four grandchildren, thanks to my sister and brother. Well, she'll have six when my brother remarries next year. Wyatt married young, had two kids, and was divorced by the time he was twenty-five. He knew, as we all did, he shouldn't have married Michelle. It's not that Michelle is a bad person, in fact, she's a really good person and a wonderful mother. They realized after a few years of marriage, the highs of a twenty-something love didn't have the longevity needed to sustain their relationship and parted amicably as friends. Michelle remarried a few years ago, and Wyatt met Raquel later that same year.

So, while my mother is determined to marry me, the baby of the family, off, she's not without the large family and loving grandchildren she's always hoped for.

"Landon, you could have worn a tie for dinner." Ah, the tie talk. This means, my mother believes the girl she's attempting to fix me up with is "the one." At least every three months or so I receive this lecture. I'm perfectly happy in my shorts and collared shirt and, if by some odd occurrence, my mother was to find my soul mate, she'll like me just the way I am.

"I could have but I'll be in suits and ties next weekend. I wanted a break. My neck needed a break," I tease my mom. She swats me with a towel while smiling.

"Ah, yes. The wedding. How is that going? Your gift?"

"The gift is about done. As for the wedding, all is well as far as I know. I think we're all just taking our orders in stride and know our primary goal is to show up, be dressed appropriately, and on time. Oh, and to not forget the groom. We can handle that."

I watch as my mom moves around the kitchen. Her movements are seamless. Grabbing a dishtowel, I watch as she wipes up a small spill before tossing the towel over her shoulder, all while chattering on about Mary or Jane, or whoever the poor girl is she's promised I'm thrilled to see tonight at dinner. My mom pauses long enough to remove one of her famous apple pies from the oven. The moment she sets the dish on a rack to cool, my dad walks into the room. He rolls his eyes at my mom and then smiles at me. Motioning toward the back door with his chin I nod and kiss my mom on the cheek before walking to the door.

"Oh, yeah. Run away. I swear you men are a pain in my ass. Go do whatever it is you do and I'll call you when Daria arrives."

"Daria?"

"Yes, the nice girl from church I invited. She's a little quiet but sweet. I've just spent the last five minutes talking about her. Seriously, Landon, it's no wonder you're still single. Selective hearing. Oh," she says, clapping her hands, "maybe she can be your plus one for the wedding."

I don't bother responding to my mom and lead my dad out of the house. We walk in silence toward my old workshop on their property. I bought a house last month and moved my shop into my garage. It's not the same as the space I've called my own since I was a kid, but it's more mine than this ever was. Regardless, nostalgia hits me in the gut the moment we pull open the door. Memories of all the pieces I've completed here roll like a movie in my head.

"Don't worry," my dad begins, "we aren't planning anything with your shop. I'll admit, I'm a bit sad to see it go."

"It's not gone, it's relocated. I had to move it eventually."

Dad sighs and pulls a beer from the mini fridge I kept in the corner next to a couch I've spent more nights on than I'd care to admit. That couch is uncomfortable and in the dead of winter as freezing as cold as it is hot in the summer. Damn fake leather.

"I know, son. I just miss having you around here all the time. Plus, it was kind of nice being in on the projects you were working on when nobody else was."

"You're welcome to come to my house anytime, Pop." I toast my dad before taking a swig from beer. We stand in silence for a few minutes before he clears his throat.

"So, this matchmaking your mother is hell-bent on. What are you thinking about that?"

"I'm thinking she's wasting her time. I'm not interested in a relationship right now. I just bought my house. I have commitments on art pieces and that big furniture project Mrs. Teller hired me for. My free time is limited."

"You should consider getting some help. Maybe find a kid you can mentor or something," Dad suggests.

"That's a good idea."

"Don't sound so surprised. I have them from time to time," Dad teases.

Over the next twenty minutes we talk about the projects I'm working on, including Ben and Piper's wedding gift. When I started working with wood, it was because I was determined to master what I couldn't finish in woodshop class. I'll never forget the look on my mom's face when she opened the wooden jewelry box I'd crafted for her. After she took it with her everywhere to brag about how talented I was, the requests from aunts and the ladies at church started. It wasn't until I found an old piece of barn wood and started messing with it that my love of creating original artwork surfaced. Most people saw the wood as trash but I saw it as, well . . . treasure. In each grain is a story. History. I love taking that and reclaiming it into something beautiful. At least what I feel is beautiful.

I am also very secretive about my projects. My mom says I have an artist's heart because I rarely share my work in progress with anyone and some have taken me up to a year to complete. I work at my pace and with what I feel. I never have a plan, but I try to give the client, or recipient, a piece that reflects them in some way.

The piece I started for Ben and Piper has taken me most of this year to complete. It's been sort of like their relationship. Like them keeping their feelings a secret for months, I kept the project a secret. The only reason Owen knew about it was because I needed help moving it one day, and I threatened to never let him have one of my mom's pies again if he told. When they chose their wedding date, I let the cat out of the bag so to speak. I knew Piper was determined to have the wedding at their house, come hell or high water, and the first thing that had to happen was finishing their fixer upper. I wanted to make sure she left space for my gift. So, I only gave her dimensions. She's had a blank wall in their house ever since.

"Well, son, it's about time we face the music. I hear the gravel and that means your one true love has arrived."

I snort in response. Love is the furthest thing on my mind. Hell, a relationship of any kind is. My first priority is getting through this wedding and then it's getting a handle on maintaining a house and my side business. Looks like I will be hiring a helper sooner than later if I have any hope of doing all of this and not losing my sanity.

Chapter 13

Daria was not my one true love. Poor thing had my mom fooled and, as much as I appreciated the effort to impress my parents, it was clear the moment she stepped out of her bright yellow sports car, Daria was not the sweet innocent young lady my mother thought she was. No, Daria was far from that.

Sure, she was nice enough. And the way she presented herself, she had . . . a lot to offer a guy. If I was interested. I wasn't. I may not be looking for a relationship but I do know obvious come-ons and a woman who displays her assets for all to see is not what I'm looking for when the time does come. My mom was startled when Daria walked in wearing a skin-tight leopard print dress with four-inch stilettos. Her breasts were pushed up in what I only assume was some sort of animal print bra and to match her almost exposed panties. My dad almost couldn't contain his laughter when my mom struggled to maintain eye contact. I get it, each time Daria reached for one of the plates of food on the table, there was a chance she'd pop right out of the top of her dress.

Daria explained that she was visiting her aunt for a few weeks while she worked out some personal problems. Her aunt demanded she dress demurely when attending Sunday services, but she hated the long skirt and high collared top she had to wear. She proceeded to explain that was why she'd worn the same outfit two weeks in a row. I guess my mom assumed she was just frugal and only had one church outfit. My poor mom. By the time she was getting dessert ready, I'd already had my thigh squeezed twice and Daria's phone number tucked in my pocket. I begged out of apple pie and ice cream, leaving my poor parents to let Daria down for me. It's the least they could do after the way she tried to stroke more than my ego under the table.

Tonight, I put the final touches on Ben and Piper's gift and made a list of duties for a helper, or apprentice as Minnie, Owen's girlfriend, called the position. She said if I call the kid, I assume it'll be a kid, an apprentice I could get away not paying someone. That seems kind of shitty. So, while I'll use the title of "apprentice" because it's better than "do the grunt work," I'll still pay whoever I find a little something. I only hope I can find someone that knows how to use my tools or, at the very least, picks up on the stuff quickly.

Once I've closed my shop, formerly known as my garage, I head into the house for a shower and a good night's sleep. I'm just about to hop in the shower when my phone signals a text message from my brother.

> Wyatt: I heard Mom's latest fix up was a bust.
>
> Wyatt: Literally.
>
> Me: Haha. You're a comedian now?
>
> Wyatt: Don't be a baby
>
> Me: When will she stop? You never dealt with this
>
> Wyatt: Nah, by the time I was your age I was knee deep in regret and debt. She gave me a pass
>
> Me: Yeah well, this bites. I don't know what her rush is
>
> Wyatt: You're her "baby boy" she wants to see you taken care of.
>
> Me: Yeah well, she may be waiting a while. I don't see it happening anytime soon.
>
> Wyatt: That's when it happens little bro. When you least expect it.
>
> Me: Whatever. I need to shower
>
> Wyatt: Raquel said she needs to talk to you about a project. I told her to back off.
>
> Me: It's fine. We'll talk. Not til after this wedding.
>
> Wyatt: Sounds good. Take care, bro. Talk later.

Just thinking of the wedding has my anxiety up. I hate dressing up, and now Piper's decided the groomsmen need to give a speech or some shit at the rehearsal. I still don't understand what we're rehearsing. We greet people, we seat them, we walk down the aisle, we get drunk. Seems simple to me. But tomorrow night we'll be gathering at Ben's parents' for a rehearsal and then Owen and I get to give a speech. Fabulous. Thankfully I'm good at improv and can usually get the crowd laughing. Keep them laughing, keep it simple, and whatever I do, talk about how pretty Piper is and what a dumbass Ben is, and I've got it in the bag.

I laugh to myself as I quickly shower off my day and my work in the shop. The sawdust from my shop swirls around the drain as I rinse off the soap and hang my head, allowing the water to pound on my neck. It's times like this I wish I had a woman to cuddle up to. To talk about my day and what's happening tomorrow. To ease the stress of giving a speech. Some nights, the single life sucks.

Okay, most nights the single life sucks. If someone came along and caught my attention I wouldn't turn down the opportunity, but I'm not sure how I'd meet a woman these days. All my friends are happily in relationships, and my work keeps me busy. Unless there's some sort of divine intervention, I don't see how I'm going to ever meet someone.

Owen is a shit. He just brought the house down with his speech. His heartfelt and emotional words, clearly Minnie helped him write the speech regardless of what he said, made my "Ben, you're a lucky bastard and better not screw this up" speech sound like child's play. I'll kick his ass later.

The evening has been fun and low key just like Ben and Piper. If you had told me a year ago we'd be sitting here at their rehearsal dinner with Ben's ex-girlfriend as the wedding coordinator, I'd have told you to share what you're smoking because that's some good shit. Not that Ben and, excuse me, "Biper" as Ashton is requiring us to call them, being together is a surprise. The reality is, there is no person better for the other than Ben and Piper are for each other. They make being together seem, well . . . seamless. If I'm lucky enough to have even ten percent of what they have, I'll be a lucky guy.

One day.

I walk to the makeshift bar and grab a cold beer before turning to observe my friends. Ben, Jameson, Owen, and I have been best friends most of our lives. The years after Ben moved away for college we didn't talk as much, but it never meant they weren't still my brothers. When he moved back last year, we picked up where we left off in high school. I've watched each of us change over the years, but the one thing that has remained the same is our bond. Today, watching each of them with the women who have chosen to put up with their crap, makes me happy for them. I tease, because I can. They're all good guys, the best, and they're damn lucky to have found love with three women who challenge and support them endlessly.

It's a great choice. For them. It's not where I am in life. While they all make it seem easy and natural, I don't understand how anyone has the time it takes to have a relationship on top of everything else they have going on.

From what I've observed over the years, relationships take a lot of work and patience. I'm a patient guy, but I think I'd prefer a relationship I didn't have to work on. I'd like a relationship that is natural and easy. Until the relationship gods create that version, I'm not interested in anything remotely close to commitment.

The Wedding Day

Chapter 14

Piper

I've been lying here for at least an hour. My bladder is about to burst, and yet I don't move. Sure, Ashton's arm across my chest is preventing much give for me to slide out of bed but, I also don't want to move. The moment I get out of this bed and start moving around, the sooner this day begins. And ends. I don't want it to end. If this day could go on forever that would make me happy.

Today is my wedding day. Today is the day my five-year-old self's dreams come true. In approximately twelve hours, I will exchange wedding vows with the man I have loved since he was a boy helping me out of the sand after I fell from the swings. Yep, at the end of this day, I will be Mrs. Bentley James Sullivan. I'm so damn excited I can hardly contain myself. And I'm determined to savor and enjoy each moment.

I think back over the last year with Ben. So many

wasted moments because I was too afraid I'd lose my best friend, his sister, Ashton. I flash to a memory of each time Ben tried to convince me otherwise. Each time he showered me with love and affection and I chose to run. To run from him and my feelings. My fear almost caused me to miss out on the greatest love of my life. Why? Because I didn't think I was worth it. And dammit, I am. I'll be forever grateful Ben believed in us enough to wait for me to get my head out of my ass.

Damn my bladder and its inability to hold off just a little longer. Nope, the time is now. I've pushed myself almost to the "emergency" part of waiting to pee. Which also means it's time for me to attempt to untangle myself from Ashton's hold. I reach my hand out, stretching as far as I can to grab my phone. With my fingertips only, I successfully slide my phone toward me and tap the screen to check the time. You've got to be kidding me. It's more last night than it is this morning.

Okay, that's an exaggeration but still. It's far too early. Sighing, I realize sleep will not come again. Also, there's the whole bladder situation, and unless I want to wake Ashton because she's lying in a puddle, I need to get moving. Quickly. Oh boy, yeah, I should've done this twenty minutes ago. When did my best friend become such a bed hog?

I manage to shimmy myself to the edge of the bed and out from under Ashton's arm with minimal disturbance. Once I've used the restroom and brushed my teeth, I pull on a sweater Ashton has hanging over the back of a chair. It's fall in Lexington, and the mornings are chilly, a hint of the pending winter in the air. I walk out of the room, quietly closing the door behind me; there's no reason for all of us to be up yet. As I pass the guest room, I stop to listen at the door for any movement from Minnie, our friend and my bridesmaid. When I don't hear anything, I continue to the kitchen.

I'm surprised to hear the last gurgles of the coffee brewing as I enter the kitchen. I make my way to the pot where I spy a mug and a note next to the pot.

Piper,

My brother insisted I have the coffee ready for you this morning. Seriously, you have him trained well. Share all the secrets! Oh, and HAPPY WEDDING DAY! Don't wake me up, I need my sleep. I've set an alarm. Enjoy the peaceful morning alone. Reflect and do all that other shit you do.

I love you, bestie sister to be!

Ash

Yes, those are tears. Bitch. She knows how I get blotchy and puffy when I cry. Laughing, I smile through the few tears I allow to spill before sucking it up. Not today. I will not be a crying mess today. I love how well Ashton and Ben both know me. I suppose that's the benefit of marrying your best friend's brother. If two people are going to know you best, it'd be them. Pouring a little creamer in my cup before filling it with the nectar of the gods, I glance at the clock to confirm the time. We still have a few hours before both my mom and Patty, my future mother-in-law, will be here for breakfast. I quickly tick off a short list of things I must do this morning: shower; not cry; go over my to-do list; not argue with my mother; not cry again; encourage

Ashton about singing; text Laurel, my friend and wedding coordinator, oh, and Ben's ex-girlfriend, to make sure she's on track for today; and most of all eat.

But before any of the to-do list can be tackled, I do as instructed. With coffee in hand, I make my way to the back deck, snuggling into one of the lounge chairs. The morning is crisp but clear. It's going to be a beautiful day. If the clouds open and drop a record amount of water on my wedding, it will still be beautiful. It will still be the day I marry my best friend, my soul mate, and the man who makes me believe not only in myself but also that good guys exist.

A good guy he is. I've been a hot mess the last month. Off and on with the flu and an overwhelming bout of nausea, I've been awful to live with. I am even sick of myself. But not Ben. Nope, as usual he's been amazing. Of course, he doesn't understand why I've also been crying non-stop. I have hardly eaten anything, and there is more than a possibility that my amazing wedding dress won't fit. There's the distinct possibility that the thing will just fall right off when I put it on. Patty and my mom have promised that won't happen. When Patty brought me soup the other day after yet another bout of vomiting, she promised to bring her sewing machine with her this morning. She wants me to put the dress on so we can confirm everything is fine. I won't do it. I only want to put the dress on once, the final moments before I leave for the ceremony. So, they'll just have to sew me right into it by hand.

I drift off in thought for a bit before I hear the sliding door open and close. I know it's not Ashton because that girl will sleep for another four hours if we let her. Which, we won't.

"Morning," Minnie says as she settles onto the lounge chair next to me.

"Good morning. How'd you sleep?" I ask before taking another drink of my now lukewarm coffee and turn to face Minnie. She's wrapped herself in a blanket with a cup of coffee in her hands, too.

"Like a rock. I've been so damn tired lately."

"Girl, I know. Me, too." I sigh.

"How are you feeling? Nervous?"

"Nope. Not at all. I'm excited. I want this day to speed up so I can be at the ceremony. But, I also want it to slow down because I don't want the day to end."

"That's understandable," Minnie agrees.

We sit and chat for a few minutes and enjoy the peaceful morning. Minnie is new to our town and our group, but she fits in perfectly. Her kind heart and sweet spirit is evident in everything she does. I'm grateful Owen found her. I love Owen Butler like a brother, but he's been kind of lost most of his life and knowing he found someone like Minnie to love and be loved by has been a blessing.

"Do you think we should wake Ashton?" I scoff at the suggestion and Minnie laughs. "You're right. How about we start on breakfast and you hop in the shower. The bride is first with the makeup artist and hair stylist."

I agree, and we return to the kitchen, each intent on filling our mugs with more coffee, only to find Ashton in the kitchen.

"What are you doing up?" I ask.

"You know I have the worst case of FOMO. I couldn't take the chance of you two bonding or some shit."

We laugh. And that's why Ashton Sullivan is my best friend. She's full of sass, but her heart is huge. I watch as she whisks eggs in a bowl, adding spices and sautéed vegetables from a pan. While Minnie and I were outside talking she started breakfast.

"Don't make a big deal about this. It's my kitchen, and if I want to start breakfast, I will. But you, Minnesota Walker, you're doing the dishes." Ashton points her finger toward Minnie, causing me to snicker. "The mothers will be here in about an hour so you two better get moving," Ashton orders.

I salute her and take my mug with me to the shower. This is going to be a great day.

Chapter 15

Ben

Waking up alone in our bed on our wedding day seems like a form of unnecessary punishment. I'd love to blame my little sister for this, but alas, it was my bride's idea. She insisted we follow tradition. Traditions are stupid. I'm also horny as hell. Piper also said a night apart would make our wedding night more electric. I don't need a night apart for our sex to be electric. Hell, just thinking about her and I'm hard as a fucking rock. But I promised to not rub one out today. She had me making vows long before the ceremony. Sneaky girl.

"Yo, are you coming down to get this day started or what, asshole?"

I ignore Owen as he shouts up the stairs. I've been awake, I'm just lying on our bed thinking. Actually, I'm trying to write my vows. Yep, the vows I have to exchange with the love of my life before our closest friends and family in a few hours. Everyone assumed I would have these done months ago. Shit, they probably expected me to have them done when I proposed last fall. They'd be disappointed.

It's not that I don't know what I want to say. It's mostly that I sound like a pussy-whipped baby. It's not too far from reality. I'm completely enamored and in love with Piper. She is everything I didn't know I wanted and was sure didn't exist. Her kindness, passion, sense of humor, and undeniable commitment to everyone she loves is only part of what makes her amazing. I've watched her at work, giving her undivided attention to each of her kindergarten students, making each one feel as if they are the most important person in the room.

Piper gives more than one hundred percent to her friends, sacrificing and supporting each of them unconditionally. It was that level of love to Ashton that almost cost us our relationship. Piper and Ashton are closer than most best friends, sisters from the heart is what they've called each other. When we were sneaking around, the stress and fear of losing Ashton as her best friend was too much for her. It wasn't a relationship she was willing to sacrifice for a romance that had only a possibility of love and forever. Thank goodness I had enough faith for both of us and believed that, eventually, Ashton's love of both myself and Piper would override any anger she had.

A true testament to Piper's unfaltering love is her unfailing support of her mother. Tessa Lawrence has never been a stereotypical mother. A single mom from almost day one, she spent more time looking for a new husband than nurturing and encouraging Piper. When we were growing up, her focus always seemed to be on appearances and molding herself into a version of the woman she thought the man she was with wanted. A chameleon of sorts. I didn't know her well but it's evident that her behavior effected not only Piper; it impacted everyone in Piper's life. Piper's insecurities, feeling of unworthiness, and horrible choice in boyfriends, before me of course, were a direct result of her mother's parenting.

As adults we see things differently. I see how young Tessa was when she had Piper. How lost and confused she was, facing parenthood alone. Does that excuse her choices or the simplistic and unworthy characteristics she made Piper believe a good man should have? No. It has, however, helped heal their relationship. Tessa has spent the last year trying to make up for her mistakes, and I think she's done a good job of that. Plus, she and I have had a few private conversations. We came to an understanding of how I expect Piper to be treated and loved. She cried, I fought tears, and she thanked me. Thanked me for loving Piper and being a good man. She also apologized. She was under the mistaken impression that being a Sullivan made me a better person than Piper. That couldn't be further from the truth. Piper is the epitome of goodness, and for that, she'll always be the better person.

I made sure Tessa understood that, to me, Piper is the ultimate package, and she created that. She may have stumbled along the way, but in the end, she has an amazing daughter who everyone loves, and she should be proud of that. She was grateful for the compliment, and I'm grateful for her stumbles along the way, because without them, Piper wouldn't be the woman she is today.

All this thinking has me wishing she was the one making all the noise downstairs. Then I could swoop down the stairs and scoop her up in my arms and kiss the hell out of her. I hesitate for a minute, knowing what I'm about to do is going to piss my sister off, and my mom will likely lecture me the moment she steps foot on my property.

Oh well, you only live once I think, smiling to myself as I tap the contacts icon on my phone.

"Your sister is going to kill you." Piper is laughing as she answers.

"I don't care, I miss you."

I hear her sigh on the other end of the line before she responds. "I know. We're pathetic. You know that, right? Like completely co-dependent. This is unhealthy. We should call the whole day off."

"No, we should have eloped so we'd be lying on a sandy beach right now."

"Then you'd have our mothers on us. Hush your mouth."

We laugh and talk for a few minutes and suddenly my vows come to me in a flash. Every memory of the past year with Piper, snippets of our childhood with her toothless grin and relentless questioning. The way she would blush and giggle when I'd say hi in the halls at school. And mostly how she looked the day I told her how much I loved her in front my parents and our friends.

"Babe, I . . ." I pause. I can't tell her I need to write my vows, she'll kill me. "I have to go. The guys are being dicks and shouting up the stairs to me.

"Oh, don't lie. I know you haven't written your vows."

"I . . . I . . . okay, fine. Sorry?" Piper giggles and then I hear a rustling before another voice comes across the line.

"Bentley James, this is your mother. You are supposed to let this woman be today. You will see her soon enough. Go do something useful and leave her to us for the day."

"Yes, Mother. May I please tell my bride goodbye?"

"Fine, but that's it. The stylist arrived, and Minnesota has poured mimosas!" My mom starts laughing, no giggling, and I assume she's already tapped into the mimosas. She shouts goodbye, and Piper returns to the phone.

"I guess we've been put in our place. It's really disconcerting how well everyone knows us," Piper says. I hear the faucet run for a minute and then the telltale signs of her brushing her teeth fill the line.

"I know, but she's right. Also, that mimosa is going to taste awful if you just brushed your teeth."

"Ben, I have been vomiting for weeks. I'm going to pass on the mimosas and pray my breakfast lasts another few hours. If that happens, I'll make sure to save my first sip of champagne so it's with you. How's that?"

"Sounds fair. I'm glad you're feeling better. I was worried." My concern has been more than I'm letting on. She had until tomorrow to stop being sick before I was forcing her to the doctor. Piper insisted the stress of the wedding and Ashton's awful sushi were the culprits. I've allowed her that excuse but I don't buy it. "Pipe?" I ask before saying goodbye.

"Yeah, babe?" The tenderness in her voice makes me smile.

"I really am sorry I didn't have my vows done. I feel like such a chick sometimes and wanted to be poetic but not crazy sappy. This is a lot harder than I thought. I can't believe you finished yours months ago."

"What? Oh, I didn't write mine," Piper teases.

"Excuse me? You said you were covered."

"I am. I'm speaking from the heart in the moment. Ben, you are my world and everyone knows that. I've been waiting for this day most of my life. There isn't anything I will say today that you don't already know. And there isn't anything you will say that I don't already know. You love me, Bentley James Sullivan. I know that as well as I know your sister is downstairs quoting Dolly Parton songs."

"Damn, you really are perfect."

"Duh, way to get on board. Now I have to go because I want to look amazing for you today, and I can't do that on my own. I love you to the moon, and I'll meet you at the altar; I'll be the one in the white dress!"

Before I'm able to respond, the lines goes dead, and I'm left sitting on my bed, staring at the wall. Damn. My dad always said I'd find a woman who challenges me, and I sure did that. She not only knows me better than I know myself, she's a hell of a lot smarter than me.

Eyeing the suit hanging on the back of my closet door, I rise from the bed and adjust the jacket on the hanger. Speak from the heart. I can do that. But before I do that, I need to go downstairs and make sure Laurel has everything she needs and the guys aren't already taking shots. We planned on taking the early part of today to fish and drink a few beers before getting ready. I suppose that's the upside of having a wedding coordinator, even if she is your ex-girlfriend.

Chapter 16

Piper

"Are you ready to put your dress on, sweetie?" My mom is standing on the other side of the door, concern evident in her voice. I've been sitting here on the toilet in Ashton's master bathroom for almost . . . yep, twenty minutes. My hair is perfectly coifed and styled, piled high and stiff as a board. I glance to the mirror and sigh relief when I take in my makeup. It's perfect. Natural with a smoky eye that will really stand out in our pictures. Ugh, but this hair. Who thought this was what I wanted? Loose waves pulled back so my long hair cascades down my back. That's what I asked for. Tight nineties prom curls piled on top of my head with *babies breath* stuck in between ringlets doesn't exactly scream "cascading."

I won't cry. I won't. If I do, that beautiful smoky eye will be for naught. I should have said something. I should have put my foot down. My friends should have said something. Nobody did. They just sat there with their mouths open, jaws practically lying on the floor. Bitches.

"Sweetie?"

"I'm here. Uh, can you get Ash and Minnie for me, Mom? I won't be long, just need a little girl pow wow." I don't bother getting up from my perch, I simply shout through the closed door. Everyone saw the monstrosity, so I'm not quite sure why I'm hiding but here I sit. Seconds later, there's a shallow knock on the door and I rise to unlock the door. I turn and walk back to my shrine of shame and sit.

"You're both fired. From best friend status and bridesmaids. This is bullshit." I glare at both Ashton and Minnie and watch as they both try to fight smiles. They look beautiful in their gowns. The tops of the dresses are different, Ashton's is strapless but gathers in an intricate design while Minnie's has straps that crisscross low on her back. Both have a thick waistband and flowing skirt. They look amazing.

Neither is sporting a horrible hair style either. Ashton is wearing her long brunette hair loosely curled with one side pulled back exposing her collarbone and shoulder. Jameson is going to lose his mind when he sees her. Minnie is wearing her blonde hair in a side chignon, giving her a classy yet simple look. Both are wearing the antique style hair combs I gifted them. I was lucky enough to come across the combs in a small shop on a trip to see my mom in Chicago.

"Wow, you both look beautiful." I sigh.

"Thanks," they say in unison.

"I can't get married like this. It's like a really bad re-run of the *Beverly Hills 90210* prom episode." Minnie gathers the skirt of her dress before kneeling in front of me. Kindness greets me when I look in her eyes. I love Minnie. She's kind and caring, always. We are always able to depend on her to come up with a resolution to any situation and still keep it positive.

"It really is, Piper. I'm sorry, but it's awful. We need to fix it," Minnie says. Wait, what?

"Huh? You're the kind one, Min! You're supposed to tell me it's not bad."

"Sweetie, it's dreadful. Let's get the plants out of your hair, and we'll fix it. We may be running a few minutes late, but we can't let you get married like this. Right, Ash?"

Both of our gazes shoot to Ashton who is standing at the sink with a wet washcloth on her neck. Oh no.

"Oh no. What's wrong? Did you catch my flu?" I ask, rushing to Ashton's side.

"What? Oh, no. I just . . . it's nothing. I just felt hot. Probably the Spanx. Let's get this hair situation handled and you married. I'm sure my brother is having a meltdown, thinking I'll talk you out of marrying his sorry ass."

"Are you sure? You look . . . well, kind of off." Ashton waves me off with disinterest, and I resign to allowing them to fix my hair.

Twenty minutes later, a lot of finger combing, an attack by the blow dryer, and I finally have the simple waves I wanted. Ashton takes my hair and pulls it from my face, fastening it with a few pins but still leaving loose tendrils to frame my face. Minnie smiles at me in the mirror, and

I simply nod before we turn toward the door. The minute the door opens, we find my mom and Patty, Ben and Ashton's mom, sitting on the bed drinking mimosas.

"Oh, Piper. You look beautiful," Patty sniffles while my mom stands next to her, hand covering her mouth.

I look them both in the eyes before replying, "You both need to suck it up. If you make me cry, and I ruin this makeup, I will kick your butts. Now, who is helping me get in that dress? I have a groom waiting."

Everyone laughs and thirty minutes later, I'm in my dress and standing alone before a full-length mirror. I knew this was my dress from the minute I found it. Originally, I wanted something simple but with a little sparkle and flare. I thought I'd found it in another dress with cap sleeves and a sweetheart neckline. But then, on a whim, I went back to the dress shop alone. As much as I wanted flare, that's not me. I'm simple. I wanted my wedding gown to reflect who I am. This sleeveless chiffon dress with a long train is more me than any other gown I tried on. Plus, the low-cut back is a fun surprise and adds a little sexiness to the simplicity of the gown. I feel beautiful and suddenly, standing here before the mirror, I realize every moment of my life has led me here, to this day when I marry my best friend.

I grab my phone from the side table and snap a picture of myself. I'm sure there will be hundreds of photos of me today but this one, one of my final photos as Piper Lawrence . . . this is something just for me.

My in-laws pulled out all the stops with a vintage Rolls Royce limousine for our drive to the ceremony also known as my house. I look at the four most important women in my life in the car with me, and I realize how grateful I am for each of them.

"I want to thank you all for everything you've done to make this day happen. I know, I know I've been difficult. I think Laurel has called me "bridezilla" more than she's called me Piper lately." Everyone laughs. "But, I've waited for this day my entire life. I wanted it to be perfect."

"It will be, honey. My son is very lucky to have you. I'm just glad he figured it out before you dumped him." I smile at Patty before reaching for the bottle of champagne on ice and filling everyone's glass and holding my glass up to clink.

We turn onto the path to our house, and I see the hustle and bustle of the pre-ceremony activities. The cars are all parked in the designated area, the ceremony area is off in the distance, but I can make out people walking in that direction. My mom pulls her phone out and taps it a few times before confirming the guys are all down at the ceremony site and the coast is clear for us to enter the house.

The car pulls up in front of the house where Laurel stands to greet us. Yes, it is strange to be friends with your fiancé's ex-girlfriend. And, it's probably more than unconventional to have her as your wedding coordinator. But, the relationship Ben and Laurel had was over long before I came into the picture, and they're friends. Best of friends, actually. My friendship with Laurel happened organically once Ben and I moved in together, and I knew for a fact she wasn't a threat. I mean, Ben has loved us both, it'd be more surprising if we didn't like each other.

"Damn, girl. You clean up nice." Laurel says after

whistling. I didn't know she could whistle like that.

"Uh, thanks? You look pretty."

"Piper, I look like a mortician. But, my job is not to look pretty, it's to make your life easy today. And then to get shitty drunk. I'm glad you insisted we have a fast-paced schedule. Plus, you know how much I love ordering people around. It's been a lot of fun. Especially your man, Ashton. Jameson is not a fan of being told what to do." Laurel laughs and Ashton snorts in agreement.

We head in the house and freshen up before the ceremony is going to start. I wasn't sure how she was going to pull off the long walk from the house to the ceremony site near the creek but Laurel has a couple of golf carts ready for us to ride in closer to the ceremony.

I know tradition is for a father to give his daughter away. I don't have a dad. I mean, I do, obviously or I wouldn't be here, but I've never had him in my life. I could have my mom give me away but that didn't seem right either. I considered having Ashton give me away but Ben vetoed that. So instead, today, I'll be walking down the aisle solo. Part of me is a little sad I won't have the tradition of my father by my side but it's just not my story and that's okay.

The moms are driven down to the ceremony first while Ashton and Minnie follow. I'm last to go so everyone is ready for me when I arrive. I'm standing in my kitchen and reminded how much I love this house. I remember when Ben brought me here the first time. He hadn't bought it yet and wanted my opinion on it. I lost the ability to talk at first. I'd had a dream most of my life about this amazing farm house with a piece of stained glass in the kitchen door. The moment he pulled up in front of the house an overwhelming feeling of home and comfort came over me. This house was what I had dreamed of. To know I live here now, that it is the home we'll raise our children, it overwhelms me sometimes. In the best of ways but still, overwhelming.

"Are you ready, Piper?" Laurel asks from the other side of the door. I nod and walk out onto the porch.

"Laurel," I say before stepping up to the golf cart. She pauses, getting in behind the wheel and looks at me.

"Yeah?"

"Thank you. For everything. For helping today, for being my friend, and as awful as someone would think this is for me to say, thank you for letting him go."

"Don't thank me. This is how it was always meant to be. I'm grateful to you both for your friendship and support this past year. This day, helping, it is the least I can do. And as for Ben, he was never really mine to keep. Now, let's get you to your groom."

As we approach the site and I see the girls standing with our flower girl, Hope, I smile. Once I'm out of the cart and sufficiently fluffed and looked over by Laurel, I turn to my wedding party. Hope, wearing a similar version of my dress with her shoulder length hair pulled back from her face, a wreath of flowers adorning her like a crown, looks up at me wide-eyed and smiling.

"Oh, Piper!" she exclaims. "You *are* a princess." I laugh because that's what she said the first time she saw me in my dress.

"Thank you, love. You look beautiful. Are you ready to show everyone how it's done?" I ask.

She nods and I look to Laurel who nods and raises her hand to signal the beginning of the ceremony. Tracy Byrd's "Keeper of the Stars" begins playing as Hope takes off before it's her turn. I shake my head because while it's not tradition, it's perfect.

Minnie waits for Hope to get at least halfway down the aisle before stepping behind the screen when Ashton turns to me. No words are exchanged between us. We both know we'll start crying, and I refuse to be puffy and blotchy for my wedding. Ashton reaches for my hand and squeezes it before she turns and begins walking toward the altar. Laurel hands me my small bouquet of wild flowers, and I take a deep breath before the music changes and I take my first step toward my future.

Chapter 17

Ben

Landon's discovery earlier still lingers in the back of my mind as I watch my dad stand at the beginning of the aisle talking to my mom and Tessa, Piper's mom. What if Piper's pregnant? I mean, we are about to get married so it wouldn't be a big deal. I mean, it *is* a big deal. A kid. Wow. I want nothing more than to start a family with Piper, but the idea of it happening is a little overwhelming. Exciting but still, overwhelming.

Memories of the last few weeks flash before my eyes, her nausea, her being beyond tired, and then her ravenous appetite. Not just for food but for me. We've blown it off as food poisoning or the flu and the wedding. But, what if it's a baby? A huge smile spreads across my face at the thought. Huge enough my mom cocks her head in my direction quizzically. I immediately replace the wattage of the smile with one that's a little less obvious.

Poker face in place, I look around me. Friends and family linger at their seats, the wedding only minutes from starting. I look toward the house, and while I can't see anything thanks to the makeshift curtains Laurel had put in place, I know just off in the distance the girls are getting ready to head this way. In less than thirty minutes, Piper and I will have exchanged vows and been pronounced husband and wife.

A hand smacks me on the shoulder, jarring me from my thoughts, and I turn to find Jameson standing next to me with a smirk on his face.

"Thinking of the wedding night?" he teases.

"Nah, just thinking of how ready I am to get through this ceremony."

"Did you finish your vows?"

"Yeah, kind of. I wrote out some words that remind me of Piper, and I'm going to speak from the heart. That's what she said she's doing, and I figure that's more our style anyway."

"You two? Off the cuff? That's not you at all." Jameson begins laughing and Landon walks up with a confused look on his face.

"What's so funny?" Landon asks.

"Ben thinks he and Piper can just say their vows without preparation. He said it's 'more their style.'" Jameson uses air quotes for the last part of his statement and his laugher increases.

"Fuck off. We can be spontaneous. It's how we got together anyway."

"I'm giving you a hard time. Don't get your panties in

a bunch. Landon, where's Owen?" Jameson inquires, looking around the crowd.

"He's helping Laurel with something before she goes up to the house for the girls. And, I think you and Piper can totally pull off random declarations of love and shit. I mean, you guys do it all the time in front of us, why not another seventy-five people?"

I flip him off before shoving him a bit. The three of us laugh and shoot the shit for a few minutes before I see some movement behind the screen, and Owen begins making his way over to us. He extends his hand and I take it in mine, shaking it as he pats me on the shoulder before taking his spot between Jameson and Landon.

"It's go time, boys," Owen says as the music begins, indicating the ceremony is beginning.

When Piper came to me a few weeks ago to talk about a few specifics with the ceremony, I didn't have much input other than the music I wanted played. We've had various love songs playing in the background for the last hour or so as people arrived and mingled. But, the songs for the ceremony, those were my choice.

I know, I'm a guy and you wouldn't expect me to have much input in something like the songs while our parents and the bridal party walk down the aisle. But, there is one song that's always held a special place in my heart. It's a song my mom used to play over and over when we were kids. My dad would always take her in his arms, regardless of where we were, or who was around, and dance with her. I remember walking in the kitchen more than once with my mom covered in flour and in my dad's embrace dancing to Tracy Byrd's "Keeper of the Stars."

So, that was the song I wanted while they all walk down the aisle and Piper and I begin the first moments of our journey into marriage. I told my dad ahead of time but not my mom. I had to tell my dad so he wouldn't try to dance with her down the aisle. He'd do it. The man has no shame.

As my dad escorts both my mom and Tessa down the aisle, one on either arm, I smile at my mom as she wipes a tear from her cheek and smiles at me. I nod my head toward her in understanding and once my dad has handed Tessa off to her boyfriend, Michael, he turns to my mom and pulls her into his arms. It's only a short dance, but it's a dance nonetheless. I laugh to myself and shake my head as they both turn to me and wink.

Our flower girl, Hope, begins her walk down the aisle, tossing rose petals along the way and waving to a few people she knows. Once she sees her parents she breaks into a huge smile that is reciprocated by her mom and dad. But, it's when she sees her uncle Jameson that she really turns on the charm. Walking up to Jameson instead of taking her place next to Piper's mom, Hope motions her finger toward Jameson, so that he squats down to her. She kisses his cheek and he pulls her into a quick hug before scooting her towards Piper's mom. A few giggles and snickers fill the air when I hear Owen curse under his breath as Minnie begins her walk down the aisle.

Jameson mocks Owen's reaction, but is cut short when my sister takes her first steps from behind the screen that blocks my bride. I hear the moment he takes in the full effect of Ashton walking towards us. I turn my head slightly to see him wiping a tear from his eye. My sister has always been beautiful but, today . . . today she looks angelic. That's saying a lot because most of the time, she's a pain in the ass. To me anyway.

Ashton keeps her eyes on Jameson, her smile growing the closer she gets. When she sees him wipe his cheek, she rolls her eyes and blows him a kiss. She's sassy but she loves my best friend, and it shows in those two actions.

As the song ends, "Canon in D" begins to filter through the speakers and the guests rise turning toward the beginning of the aisle where Piper stands. My breath hitches as I take her in. Her beautiful auburn hair is down and a slight breeze is enough to pick up the pieces around her face. She looks ethereal.

I don't bother to wipe away the tears that fill my eyes and spill down my cheeks. What's the point? Everyone here is wiping their eyes. Piper is the epitome of beauty in her white gown and bouquet of simple wildflowers. Like Piper, her gown is elegant and perfect. She looks at me, only me. Her gaze never leaves mine. I hope she sees how much I love her, how much she means to me. My love and adoration for her knows no bounds.

When she is about halfway down the aisle, I step away from my designated spot and walk toward her. Confusion marks her face as I approach, but she doesn't stop walking until I'm in front of her, taking her hand.

"Hey, baby."

"Ben what are you doing?" she whispers.

"Meeting you halfway. We do this together from here

on out. Side by side, as partners."

Piper smiles and I lean down to kiss her, but she turns her cheek. "No way, mister. Save that for the big finale."

I laugh and take her hand to lead her to the altar. Our guests wait for the pastor to offer permission to sit. Once everyone is settled in, the ceremony begins. Pastor Timmons is a family friend and has known all of us most of our lives. He's able to personalize and bring a level of familiarity to our ceremony that's exactly as we hoped it would be. A few tears are shed by all, but it's the laughs that dominate the ceremony. When it's time for us to recite our vows, Piper turns to hand Ashton her bouquet as Pastor Timmons secures the rings from Jameson.

Piper and I face one another, holding hands and smiling. I want to move this part along. The faster we get through this, the sooner I can kiss her.

"Ben, Piper," Pastor Timmons pauses, looking at us pulling our gazes from each other and toward him. "Marriage is more than love and commitment. Marriage is about partnership, understanding, and forgiveness. Piper, we know Ben is probably going to drive you crazy from time to time." The guests snicker and Piper nods her head in agreement. "And Ben, Piper is sure to frustrate you on the very rare occasion." I agree and Piper smacks me playfully before taking my hand again. "But, it is in those moments that you will choose how you react. You will choose respect and love above all other emotions."

Piper and I nod in agreement, and I watch as Piper takes a deep breath. She knows this is when we begin our vows.

"It is my understanding that you are both prepared to recite your own vows, is that correct?" Pastor Timmons asks, and we nod in agreement. I remember from our meetings with the pastor and the rehearsal that I am to go first.

Taking a deep breath, I begin to declare my feelings for my future wife in front of all our family and friends.

Chapter 18

Piper

I am freaking out. I didn't write any vows. I wrote some words on a piece of paper and then stared at it, willing something epic to pour out of me. Nothing. Nada. Zilch. And that paper? With the words? I left it in my purse. In the house. I was so flustered before we left the house for the ceremony I forgot to grab it from my purse. I was kidding when I told Ben I was going to "wing it" but looks like the joke's on me.

Now as I watch my amazing fiancé, soon to be husband, clear his throat to begin his vows, I hope I'm able to hold it together long enough to fly by the seat of my pants when it's my turn.

"Piper," he begins while tightening his grip on my hands, his nerves evident. "Damn, girl. You blow me away. That's not poetic or even romantic, but it's the truth. I've known you most of your life but last year when I saw you sitting on that bar stool, waving your arms around dramatically, you captured my interest and never let go. I didn't know it that night but I should have, you not only captured my interest but stole my heart. My vow to you is to always respect and honor you. To hold your needs and feelings to a higher standard than my own, and never let you feel any less than cherished. I look forward to creating more memories with you, memories blanketed with laughter and love. But mostly," Ben pauses and takes a deep breath, closing his eyes before opening them and looking at me. His eyes are full of love and I melt a little on the spot.

"Mostly, I look forward to creating a family with you. I can't wait until the day our children run around this land playing and teasing. I look forward to the day I hear a smaller version of you fill the silence with laughter. I told you once that your voice is like honey. The sweetest and thickest honey. That holds true. And, as much as I'll still listen to you recite the phone book to me, reading bedtime stories to our children will be the highlight of my life. Piper, I promise to always put the toilet seat down, throw my laundry as close to the hamper as possible, and keep the bed warm." Ben earns a few chuckles from the guests and me.

"I love you, Piper. You loving me makes me a better man, and I can't wait for the rest of our lives to show you how much I cherish you."

I unclasp my hand from Ben's and attempt to wipe my tears away without smearing my makeup. A handkerchief appears from my side as I note Ben's dad extending his hand toward me. I smile and take the offered blessing and smile my gratitude. He doesn't know what a saving grace this is because it's about to get really messy when I have to say my vows.

"Piper," Pastor Timmons encourages me. Taking a deep breath, I look up at Ben through my lashes and all my worries melt away.

"Bentley. When I was five years old, you were my knight in shining armor. You offered a shy little girl a helping hand, and I'm not sure you knew in that moment what you were getting yourself into. For years I watched you from afar, wishing you'd look at me differently. You didn't." Ben shifts his feet uncomfortably, but I squeeze his hand reassuringly.

"And, I'm so grateful. I wouldn't change a single moment we've had together. Even if my teenage self wished we had been together most of our lives, I'm glad we weren't. If I've learned anything in this last year, it's that being loved by you is the greatest gift I have ever been given. I would never have appreciated the depths of true love before now. Thank you for coming home. Not only home to Lexington, but to me. You, Bentley James Sullivan, are my home. In your heart is where I belong, and I will never take that for granted. I vow to honor and cherish the love you give me and bestow the same upon you and our children. And, as you wished for a smaller version of me, I wish upon every star in the night's sky for a little Bentley who treats every person in his life with love and respect just like his daddy."

I'm sobbing by the time I say the word "daddy" and Ben unclasps our hands and pulls me toward him, his left hand on my waist while his right wipes the tears from my cheek. He looks to the pastor and whispers "Can we move this along, Pastor?"

Pastor Timmons smiles and nods. He says a few words I don't really hear. Everything I've needed to hear and everything I've needed to say having been said, I stare at Ben. The rest of the world fades away as I hold his gaze. I know the minute the pastor has pronounced us husband and wife because the biggest grin takes over Ben's face and he tugs me to him in a passionate kiss.

His kiss speaks of forever and always. It holds promises for today and all the tomorrows that follow. It is a kiss that evokes every emotion and feeling we share, and I succumb to it naturally. My hands loop around his neck as he lifts me from the ground. Okay, so maybe this kiss is a little more than feelings because the way he's kissing me, he's about ready to make those future babies we talked about right now.

The sounds of claps, whistles, and clearing throats finally filter through my love-filled haze and we pull apart. Ben is still holding me off the ground and now we're both laughing. Once he sets me down, we turn to face our guests as Pastor Timmons announces us as Mr. and Mrs. Bentley James Sullivan. The speakers crackle as the first chords of "Just Like Heaven" by The Cure begin. I look at Ben, and we both start laughing as I reach for my bouquet from Ashton and turn to make our way back down the aisle. Sure, it's not the most common recessional song, but it's fun and upbeat.

As we approach the end of the aisle, Laurel is there with an awaiting golf cart and a huge smile on her face.

Happiness radiates off her. She's happy for us.

"You guys are amazing. And screw you both for making me cry. Now, go up to the house, freshen up, knock one out, whatever you need to do," she says, shooing us to the golf cart. She knows as much as we do that there will be no "knocking one out" when we get to the house. The next cart will house the bridal party and Pastor Timmons so we can sign the marriage certificate and freshen up for photos. The photographer has already staged an area for us to take the photos but the actual signatures will be done in the kitchen, the license placed in a waiting envelope and put in my mother-in-law's bag for mailing.

Ben and I head straight for our bedroom, where we kiss and relish in the quiet for a few moments. I quickly freshen up while he uses the restroom and sends Ashton up to help me with my dress while I use the restroom. We may be married but I'm not quite ready for Ben to hold my dress while I pee.

Once everyone has relieved themselves, taken a celebratory shot of whiskey, and the marriage license is signed, we head outside for the photographs. The photographer has a list of the photos I hoped to capture and is, thankfully, quick with the process. Laurel appears halfway through the picture taking to bring us snacks and demands we all eat something to keep from getting "college level wasted" tonight. We all laugh, but she does know us well. Everyone willingly takes the food offered, and sure, another shot of whiskey, before going back to picture taking. That's when I stop Laurel and ask the photographer to add a few unplanned shots to the list. Pulling Laurel into a hug I force her to take a few pictures with Ben and me.

As soon as the pictures are done, the girls and I make another bathroom stop before meeting the guys outside. Before we exit the kitchen, I look at the clock and confirm we are on schedule. I want to get all this official wedding business done quickly so we can have a good time.

Before Ashton hops in the golf cart, I stop her to make sure she's doing okay before singing. "I'm golden, sister. I have Jameson here, and while the song is for you guys, he'll be the one I sing to. It grounds me. Don't worry."

"I'm not worried, I just care." I hope she knows I mean that. If she chose not to sing, I would be okay with that, too.

Laurel stops our golf carts just a few feet from the tent where the reception is taking place. I hear music playing and the guests laughing and talking. I love that everyone here knows one another and they are enjoying themselves.

"Laurel, you need some of this," Landon declares, shoving a flask in Laurel's face. I half expected her to wave it off, but instead she grabs the offering and throws back a hearty swig.

"Thanks, Landon. I did need that. This coordinator job is not the cakewalk I had expected. Someone has us on a tight-ass schedule." She's teasing but everyone agrees just the same. Brats.

"Y'all ready to do this?" Laurel asks, and everyone agrees. Since I only have two bridesmaids, Landon is going to walk out with Hope. I felt horrible but he offered and said the two of them have a plan. I have no idea what that is, but I can't wait to see it.

The DJ's voice fills the air as he gets the crowd going with some party music before the song we chose to walk into the reception begins to play. One of my favorite party songs of all time is "Celebration" by Kool and the Gang. Sure, it was popular before I was even born, but it's iconic and exactly how we want to kick off our reception. Landon and Hope are first to enter, and I peek around a corner to find them doing a dance routine. Hope is shimmying along with her hands in the air and spinning. Landon is doing an awkward shuffle with his hands tucked like he's preparing for a boxing match. It's adorable and hilarious. We all laugh and Jameson's sister, Julia, is up and out of her seat with her phone poised in Hope's direction. No doubt she's documenting this for future blackmail in Hope's teenage years.

The couples follow Landon and Hope leaving Ben and me alone for a moment. "This may be the last time we have a minute alone for the rest of the night," Ben says, pulling me to him. As he does, the song we've chosen to walk in to fills the air and everyone is clapping and laughing. "Brick House" by the Commodores, another surprise song but perfect for the party that's about to take place.

"Kiss me then, I'd hate to sacrifice these minutes talking." I no sooner finish my statement than Ben is kissing me passionately. Suddenly, we're pulled apart by Laurel and shoved into the tent where everyone is laughing. We look at each other and shrug. Dancing our way to the head table, it isn't long before the rest of the room is dancing along to the song and I couldn't be happier.

This is how I always envisioned my wedding - a night with our closest friends and family, full of laughs and love with Bentley Sullivan next to me. This day simply proves dreams do come true, and if you really believe, the good guy does get the girl.

Chapter 19

Ashton

I am grateful for Piper's demand that all wedding festivities move along at a quick pace. I will be singing for the first dance in about fifteen minutes. She wanted to do speeches and the dance before dinner was served because once those are out of the way it's just partying and cake. Everyone in this tent will stop what they're doing for cake. But, I'm mostly grateful because I think if I ate any more than the snacks Laurel gave us earlier, I'd be tossing my cookies right now.

Stress and nerve-induced anxiety are part of my life. I've worked hard these last few months to find coping tools to deal with it. I've been doing okay, but today I'm beyond stressed. It's more than the fact that almost every person in this room is either related to me or has known me most of my life. I suppose this is what happens when your brother is the groom; every aunt, uncle, cousin, and distant relative shows up in one room, or tent in this case.

My mom is thrilled to have most of our family togeth-er and for that reason I'm happy for her. But the cousin I haven't seen since our family reunion fifteen years ago is side-eyeing me like I killed her puppy. I didn't. She needs to get over it.

"Babe," Jameson whispers in my ear. His breath sends shivers down my spine, and I send up a little prayer that this feeling never goes away. I hope and pray his voice and the feeling of his breath on my skin never stop sending bursts of lust and desire through my body. As much as I'm enjoying the pooling of lust in my core, I'm looking for-ward to this night ending. A few days ago, while search-ing his desk for paper, I found the printout from the hotel he booked in Nashville. My guy is planning a getaway for us, and it includes my bucket list item number five—the Country Music Hall of Fame. I'm so excited. At least, I hope it's the Hall of Fame. What if he doesn't know that's on my bucket list? I'll be happy with whatever he plans, but hopefully he listens when I ramble about my bucket list items.

Oh, he's still lingering at my ear. That's my sweet spot. Damn, that tickles.

"Hmm," I sigh as I lean into his side.

"Why is that woman giving you dirty looks?"

I look to where he's motioning and confirm my sus-picion as to who might be glaring at me. "That's my cous-in, Molly. She's pissed because I killed Sparky," I offer non-committedly while taking a drink of my water.

"Sparky? Who or what is Sparky?" Jameson asks

thoroughly confused.

"Her fish. She's ridiculous." I look to where Molly is staring and offer her an over-exaggerated wave and smile before turning to Jameson. "When we were kids, she had this damn gold fish she took everywhere. I mean everywhere. Like it was her damn toy. Anyway, we had a family reunion and had to share a room. I swear that fish was starving and one day I'd had enough. So, I may have dumped the container of food in his bowl." Jameson starts laughing harder than necessary. "Hey, he was *starving to death*. Molly was a horrible fish mom. I'm sorry Sparky overate, but I was worried about him."

Jameson pulls me toward him and places a kiss to my temple, still laughing. I nestle in and let him hold me for a few minutes before Laurel motions to us that it's time for our speeches. Great. I have to do that, too. I pull back from Jameson to allow him space to stand and take the offered microphone. He clears his throat before speaking.

"Good evening everyone. I'm going to keep this short because I know there are three things in this world that scare me. One is my beautiful girlfriend, Ashton Sullivan, whom most of you know. When she's pissed off, boy howdy, it's enough to send a man running. Trust me I know." He turns and winks at me and I fake scowl. It's true. I am scary. "The second, that's Laurel. Laurel is the beautiful woman in black who has been keeping this day running. She's also a very focused task master and if I run over in my speech, she may run me over. And finally, the third person I'm afraid of is our blushing bride, Piper Lawren—Sullivan. Wow, that sure does have a nice ring to it, doesn't it?" Jameson looks over at Piper, who is beaming. Yep, Sullivan is a perfect fit for her.

"Anyway, as most of you know, I've been best friends with Ben since we were little. He's like a brother to me, and his friendship has been a blessing. And a curse. It's hard being best friends with the best guy in town, but that's who he is. Then, there's Piper. Sweet, smart, and kind Piper. And patient. I mean, we all know how patient she's been. Twenty years patient." The crowd laughs and Piper nods her approval as Ben leans in and kisses her temple, pulling her closer to his side.

"Last year Ben called me and told me he was moving home. I was excited to have my best friend come home. We were going to camp, fish, hell maybe even get some hunting in. But then I took him to Country Road, and he spotted a cute little redhead and that plan went to shi . . . we're all friends here, Hope, earmuffs," he instructs, looking to his niece who covers her ears. "Shit. It all went to shit the minute he spotted Piper across the bar. Best loss of my plans ever. If ever there were two people who belonged together, it's Ben and Piper. So, raise your glass with me. To Ben and Piper, may your days be joyful and your nights playful. Cheers!"

The entire room clinks glasses and offers a cheers and Jameson looks down at me before placing his champagne glass on the table and offering me his hand to stand. I take his offered hand and push my chair back a little before standing. Taking the microphone from Jameson, I turn to the crowd and smile.

"Well, that's a tough act to follow. I mean, there was

swearing and everything. Good job, babe. This is my family, way to pull out all the stops," I joke. My comments are greeted with laughs, my dad's the loudest. I see he's also been hitting the whiskey.

"I'm going to keep this short too. Not because I'm scared of anyone, y'all know I can take them both." Nods from everyone around me fill me with a little pride and my smile widens before I continue. "Piper, when you used to crush on my brother as a kid, I thought you were nuts. He was so annoying, well, he still is, but whatever, he's your problem now." The crowd laughs, causing me to pause. My voice changes as I get a little more serious. "Then something changed. You changed. I didn't see it at first and when I realized the reason for your change was my brother, I was taken aback. Most of you know they kept their relationship from me for months, but looking back I see it all. You two, you're like a perfect puzzle. Apart you're just pieces waiting to find their counterpart. But, together you make a beautiful picture. I'm so glad my idiot brother finally gave me the only gift I've ever wanted, making you my sister."

Piper's eyes glisten as she mouths "I love you" before I continue, "Piper, thank you for loving my brother. For seeing the wonderful man he is and showing him love in its truest form." I pause as the threat of tears is imminent. "The two of you are what fairy tales are made of, and I wish you countless years of happiness. Cheers."

Piper takes a sip of her champagne before standing and walking around the guys to hug me. She's sniffling, and that's my undoing. I begin crying. I've done so well. It's been at least six hours since I've cried last. I thought it was behind me. I know it's not. I know it's only the beginning. These overwhelming emotions are exhausting.

"Thank you, Ash."

"Don't thank me yet. I still have to get through this song. I love you, Pipe. Never doubt that. Sisters for life, now." I pull back and smile at her. She's laughing, and I join her for a few seconds before nudging her back toward her seat.

Instead of handing the microphone back to the DJ, I turn it off and set it on the table as I take my seat. I drink more of my water and sit back for a minute contemplating whether a bathroom stop is necessary before the first dance song. If I go this will mark the tenth time today and the fourth time in this dress. A dress, I may add, that isn't the easiest for so many potty breaks. I shrug off the idea and look up to find Laurel with the DJ. I know she's ensuring he has the music cued for the dance. Once they finish speaking she motions for me to join them. The DJ is up on a bit of a mini stage. There isn't much room but plenty for me to stand up higher than the floor and out of the way.

I kiss Jameson on the lips and linger for the briefest moment before pulling away. His eyes are open, watching me. His eyebrows shoot up like he's realized something, but I see Laurel walking towards us. He opens his mouth to say something, but Laurel speaks before he has a chance.

"Ashton, are you ready?" Laurel asks. I nod in response but look back at Jameson. He looks pale.

"Are you okay? You don't look good. Maybe lay off the whiskey until after dinner." He's not speaking but his mouth is opening and closing as if he is. "Hey," I say more urgently, "What's wrong?"

"You didn't drink your shots."

"No, I didn't. It's no biggie. I need to go sing. Please stand over there." I point to the end of the long table we're sitting at. "I need to be able to look at you. I'm calm on the outside, but it's like a damn hurricane of emotions inside."

"You're not drinking your champagne."

"What is wrong with you? Babe, please stay with me for five minutes. Once the song is done, we'll eat and you'll feel better. I promise," I say, placing a chaste kiss on his lips before grabbing the microphone and heading to the spot next to the DJ designated for me.

"Ladies and gentlemen. While the servers are bringing around your salads, we invite you to help us welcome Mr. and Mrs. Bentley Sullivan to the dance floor for their first dance. Tonight, the maid of honor, Ashton Sullivan, will be singing."

A round of applause welcomes Ben and Piper to the dance floor. Ben dramatically spins Piper as the opening chords of "When You Say Nothing At All" begin. I take a deep breath and seek out Jameson. I need him to ground me. I never realized how much until now. There's so much change going on in all our lives, and I think it's hitting me like a ton of bricks. This feels like more than nerves from singing in front of everyone.

My voice is quiet as I begin singing. Thankfully, that isn't far off from the Alison Krauss version of the song which is Piper's favorite. I look to Ben and Piper as they embrace one another, whispering and smiling. Piper has one hand on Ben's shoulder, pulling him into her as her other hand is linked with Ben's behind her back. Dancing like this, they look like one person, perfectly molded together. My thoughts go to Jameson as I seek him out.

He's standing where I asked him to, but the look on his face is perplexing. I come to a pause in the lyrics and look at him quizzically. He looks from my face to my stomach, and I instinctively drop my hand protectively to my lower abdomen.

He knows.

How? Nobody does. I didn't tell Piper or Minnie. I almost called my mom, but she's not who I should tell first. I was scared. I am scared. This isn't the plan. We haven't been together even a year. Not that it should matter, he's it for me. He always has been. My life changed for the better the day I fell in love with Jameson Strauss. I could have done without the years of not having that love in my life, but I have it now. I never doubt his feelings for me, never. His love is honest and true. It is obvious, and it is pure. My eyes fill with tears as he looks again from my face to where my hand rests and then back up. I smile as the first tear escapes and nod.

I watch as his expression morphs from bewilderment to pure joy. He lets out a shout that matches his expression and startles most everyone as he runs to me. Thankfully, the song is almost over and I'm able to hand the microphone to the DJ and allow the instrumental ending to close out the dance. Jameson scoops me up in his arms and spins me around.

"Oh shit, I shouldn't do that." I laugh as I grab his head with my hands and pull him to me for a kiss. I love this man, every day and all day. He is it for me and now for our baby. That's right, I'm pregnant. Unplanned, unwed, and not a care in the world.

After a few minutes of him holding me in the air and kissing me, he breaks free and sets me down. Taking my hand in his, he pulls me outside and away from the crowd. No words are spoken as he takes me down to the ceremony site. He motions for me to sit down in the one of the chairs and I do. And I wait while he stands there staring off toward the creek.

Jameson's initial reaction made me believe he's as excited for this baby as I am. Standing before me, his brow is furrowed, his lips are pinched into a hard line, and his hands are running through his hair. Maybe he's not as excited as I thought he was.

Chapter 20

Jameson

That damn test has been on my mind all day. I looked at each of the girls as they walked down the aisle for the ceremony and didn't see any signs of pregnancy. Then, I was caught up in the celebration and happiness of Ben and Piper that I forgot for a minute. While Ashton was giving her speech, the pieces started falling into place but I thought for sure she would have told me if the test was hers.

When she stood and walked toward the DJ to begin her song, each moment of the last few weeks flashed before me like a silent movie—all the crying, her moodiness, and her exhaustion. We'd chalked it all up to the stress of the wedding but it isn't. It's a baby.

Our baby.

As she began singing, she twisted toward the DJ to motion something and I saw it. A slight pooch—I'll never

ever admit that to her. The lyrics of the song, the emotion in her voice, and the way she subconsciously moved her free hand to her stomach, it all felt like it was her telling me about the baby. Suddenly, not taking the shots of whiskey or drinking her champagne made sense. The exhaustion, her bigger than normal breasts. All of it. As soon as she caught my gaze resting on her stomach, her eyes grew in shock.

The funny thing is, I wasn't freaked out. Sure, when Landon found the test this morning my instinct was to be negative about it. This isn't how it's supposed to go. Well, traditionally anyway. But, Ash and I aren't traditional. We've been in love with each other for years and ignored it. We spent more time trying to hate each other than accepting the truth and being together. That's why when it all sunk in the thought of her pregnant with our child, I instantly felt relaxed and at peace. Seeing her stand before me, doing what she loves and was born to do while protectively holding her hand where our baby is nestled, overwhelmed me. The feelings were more than I could have ever imagined.

"Are you angry?" she asks. Angry? How could she think that? Oh, because I haven't said a word. Dickhead move.

"Angry?" I ask, kneeling before her, taking her hands in my own. "Baby, I'm not angry. I'm ecstatic. Over the moon. Fucking stoked!" I say, causing her to smile.

"Are you sure? I mean, I didn't plan this, but it's our baby, J." Tears start flowing like a faucet from her eyes, and I place a hand on either side of her face, forcing her to look at me.

"I have never been surer of something in my life. That's not true. There's something else, but that'll have to wait until next week. One big thing at a time. We don't want to overshadow Ben and Piper."

"I don't know what that means. Oh, my goodness, are you embarrassed to have a baby momma?"

"What?" What the hell is she talking about? "No. Never. I'm so fucking happy to have a baby momma, but it's just this is all so unexpected," I say, pulling my hands from her head and standing. Taking a step back, I look up toward the tent. I see our friends standing just outside, waiting. They know what happened. Of course, they do. Ben, Landon, and Owen know about the test. By the way I reacted they had to have figured out it's Ashton's test.

"Do it, J!" Ben shouts from where he's standing, and I watch as my sister, his parents, and my folks step outside. Shit, do I? I look down to where Ashton was sitting, and she's gone. I look up to see her walking away from me, her shoulders shaking because she's crying. Everyone important to us are here, it seems dumb to miss this opportunity.

"Babe," I say, reaching for her hand and stopping her. She doesn't turn around to face me but stops walking. I put my hand to my right pocket. The box is there. I don't know why I grabbed it earlier and put it in my pocket, but I did. Maybe I knew earlier this would happen. I really didn't plan it. I don't want to take away from Ben and Piper, but he did just give me permission, right?

Throwing caution to the wind, I drop to one knee and tug Ashton to look at me. "Baby, please turn around." When she does, she gasps, her free hand going to her mouth and her head turning toward the group gathered near the tent, Ben and Piper in the forefront. Piper is standing in front of Ben with her hands over her mouth. She and Ashton are so similar in their reactions, it'd be amusing if I wasn't freaking the fuck out right now.

"Ashton, I am far from embarrassed by anything about you. This just caught me off guard, I had this grand plan for next week. I told your dad . . ." She cuts me off before I can continue.

"You talked to my dad?"

"Of course, I did. I asked the most important man in your life for permission to marry you."

"You didn't. Oh my God. You don't need my dad's permission, you dope. You need *mine*." I laugh; that's my girl.

"Yes, well, I also need your dad's because I respect him and wanted him to know how much I love you. He of course warned me of this exact conversation, and he'll be happy to know he was right, and I was wrong. I didn't think you'd get sassy with me on one knee."

"Clearly, you've forgotten who you knocked up," she teases.

"May I?" I ask, gesturing to my knee in the dirt. She nods.

"Ashton Marie Sullivan. I could go into a big speech about how we're meant to be together, how much I love you, and how I'm a better man since you've agreed to be with me. But I won't. You know all of that and tell *me* on a regular basis." She snorts and I smile. "What I will say is, I love you. With all that I am and all that I'll ever be, you complete me in more ways than one. Your drive, your passion, your kind heart, and your unfaltering commitment to our friends and family amaze me on a daily basis. It would be my greatest honor if you would let me call you wife and marry me."

"You did not just say "call you wife"! Dear Lord, Jameson," she chastises with a smile and eye roll. "Get off the ground." I do as instructed.

"I'm going to get fat. I'm going to be moody and cry a lot. There will be cravings. Do you get what I'm saying here?" I mimic a bobble head as she pauses. "I'm a lot to handle, but you seem to handle me well. And of course there's the fact that there is no other person in this world I could love. You're it for me, Jameson Strauss. End game. You and me. Well, and this nugget. Who, I believe, was conceived thanks to that game of naked Truth or Dare you challenged me to."

Ah, yes," I pause tapping my chin in thought. Naked Truth or Dare, I remember that night. It was an excellent night. Messy but excellent. "Well, it's lucky for you," I say, pulling the ring from the box and holding it up to the moonlight, "you're it for me, too. What do you say? Wanna make an honest man of me?"

"Nothing would make me happier."

I place the ring on Ashton's finger and scoop her up into my arms as I kiss her. This wasn't how I envisioned proposing. It surely wasn't the order in which I expected our future to play out, but that's par for the course with us. Nothing is ever as we plan it and that's perfect for us.

We welcome our families and friends to congratulate

us. Ashton's mom pulls her into a tight hug and then looks at her knowingly. When Ashton nods her head in acknowledgement, Patty begins to cry. Confirmation that we're expecting leads to more congratulations from everyone. It's only after about ten minutes that I realize we've all abandoned the reception. I tell everyone to head back in and hold Ashton back with me. She's beaming and holding her hand to her abdomen again. I look at her quizzically to which she mimics.

"What?" she inquires with a raised brow.

"You're beautiful, you know that?"

"Oh stop, I've got the ring on, you don't have to butter me up."

I laugh because that's such an Ashton comment to make. I pull my phone from my pocket pull her hand up to take a picture before tugging her in for a selfie.

"What are those for?"

"So, we don't forget this night," I say sheepishly as she steps into me, her arms going around my waist as she looks up at me.

"I could never forget this day. October twenty-first will go down in my life history books as one of the single most important days of my life. Never doubt that, J. Ever. Now, your child is starving, and we must be fed."

I know not to argue with a woman but especially a pregnant woman and take Ashton back to the tent for dinner. We're greeted with our own round of applause and the DJ playing "Going to the Chapel." Ben and Piper are ridiculous. And fantastic. This is their day, and they've just made a huge part of it our day.

Chapter 21

Owen

I wasn't surprised by how beautiful Minnie looked today. She sent me a selfie earlier after she was dressed. I knew then how amazing she looked. I knew the dress fit her perfectly, and the minute I saw her I was going to think of ten different ways to get her out of the dress. But, what I wasn't prepared for was the way I felt when I saw Minnie walking down the aisle. She took my breath away. Her beauty is only part of it. The fact that she's here, with my friends, accepted as one of our own within months, and she chooses me. Well, it was a little overwhelming. I mean, I wasn't a pussy like Jameson and crying.

Okay, that's bullshit. There was maybe one tear. Or two. What can I say? We're sensitive dickheads. During the ceremony, I caught Minnie looking my way a few times, and I sent her one of my panty-melting smiles. This smile is not my opinion, it's a fact. It's a smile I can send toward my girl and she's dropping her panties, ready for more than just smiles.

"Hey, handsome. Ready to spin me around that dance floor?" I turn to the voice of my angel. The woman who has completely transformed my life and yet encourages me to stay true to who I am and never tries to change me.

"Sure am. How's Ash?" I ask.

"She's great. A little overwhelmed I think. The baby makes the last few weeks with her make so much more sense. And the number of times she's needed a restroom today." The DJ announces for the wedding party to take their place on the dance floor. We're improvising since we were supposed to join Ben and Piper during the end of the first dance, but then Jameson figured out Ashton was pregnant. As soon as he scooped her up in his arms, I'll admit my stress level dropped about fifty percent. I know Minnie and I are careful, but there was that lingering thought all day after Landon found the test that we hadn't been as careful as I thought.

I pull Minnie into my arms, and she settles in with her head resting on my shoulder, her face toward my own. We dance for a minute in silence, allowing the moment to wrap itself around us in complete peace.

"Ashton told me you guys found the test earlier," Minnie whispers as she pulls her head from my shoulder and peers up at me through her long lashes.

"Landon did," I confirm.

"Were you scared? I'm surprised you didn't call me."

"I didn't want to ruin the day, and I know we're careful." I don't really like where this conversation may be headed. Minnie and I have only been together a few months and we are living in a house that currently has a bed, a television, and two bean bag chairs. We aren't exactly ready for kids.

"I know we're careful but things happen. I feel like this is something we should talk about. Do you want children?" Her eyes are wide as she stares at me, waiting for me to respond. I've never given kids much thought before Minnie. I never thought I'd meet someone who would have me looking at a future. A future that may include a couple kids, a dog, and an SUV. No minivan for this guy.

"Minnesota," I say with a quirked brow as I wrap both hands around her waist and tug her closer to me. The moment our bodies connect, my buddy in my pants hardens. Inappropriate fucker.

"Don't 'Minnesota' me, Owen. You can't charm me with that deep voice and your cock. Answer the question." Feistiness. It's one of my favorite things about my girl.

"I'll be honest, I never gave it much thought. I had a shit childhood, and I always assumed I'd be a shitty father."

Minnie's gaze drops and her shoulders collapse as if she's giving up. I lift her chin up so she's looking at me. The song changes but stays slow. Most of the guests have joined us on the dance floor and I glance around, taking in the people around us before continuing.

"I never gave it much thought because I didn't think I would ever meet someone I wanted to have that with. Then, baby, then I met you. Nothing in this world would make me happier than having kids with you."

"Really?" she asks, a tentative smile appearing.

"Yes, really. I don't think we're there yet. I mean, I just bought the house, and we haven't even bought a couch yet. Maybe we should furnish our home before we think about nurseries and shit." A full smile takes over Minnie as she begins running her fingers through the hair at the nape of my neck.

"But, we can practice, right? I mean, that's not out of the cards."

"Yes, my little sex kitten. We'll practice so much you'll be sick of me."

Minnie and I dance for a few more minutes before my dad and his girlfriend, Barb, approach us. I told Minnie I had a shitty childhood and assumed I'd be a shitty dad. That's a little unfair to my dad, but it's true. He was far from father of year. Hell, he was barely a father some days. But, we've turned a corner in the last few months, and while we have a long way to go, I understand him more and I look forward to building a friendship with him.

"We're going to head out soon, son, but I wanted to see if I can interest this lovely lady in a quick dance before we do." My dad motions toward Minnie who smiles and steps out of my embrace.

"Why Lee Butler, I'd be honored," she says with a curtsy. These two are bosom buddies. The minute my dad, a lifelong Minnesota Twins fan, learned the woman I was dating was named Minnesota, he was head over heels for her. Barb and I sit on the sidelines while the two of them talk about random trivia, and my dad tries to explain the rules of baseball to Minnie.

"Barb, shall we?" I ask, extending my hand. Barb

accepts my offered hand, and we dance for the remainder of the song before an old Brooks & Dunn song starts playing and we turn our slow dance into a two-step.

After a few dances with Barb and my dad, Minnie and I walk them out of the tent to say goodbye. It was nice of Piper and Ben to include our parents on their day. I know Minnie had hoped Dakota would have been here, but she's still adjusting to the loss of her husband, being a single parent to two small girls, and being home from rehab. Dakota and I haven't always seen eye to eye but I like her a lot and have faith that soon she'll grow to love me. I can understand why a wedding would be hard for her. I can't imagine it's easy to celebrate someone else's forever when hers was cut short so recently.

By the time the wedding portion of the night is over, many of the guests have departed, and all that's left are friends, some of Ben and Ashton's aunts and uncles, and a few cousins. I'd say we're about to kick it up by the way everyone is heading to the bar.

I spy Minnie talking to Piper and Ashton, her hand on Ashton's stomach. Women. Ash is probably six seconds pregnant, and they're likely planning her baby shower, and I guess, bridal shower. I shake my head at their predictability and walk toward where the guys are standing.

I look in the direction they're all staring and see two of Ben's teenage cousins trying to sneak a few bottles from the large bins filled with ice and beer. We stand and watch in silence. Waiting. Then it happens, and we start laughing.

Taylor swoops in behind the kids and grabs them each by their shirt collar and hauls them away. We all break out in laughter, bent over with tears running down our faces.

"Those kids are probably shitting themselves right now," Landon says.

"Serves them right. Little bastards," Ben snorts.

"Ah come on guys. We were their age once," I remind them.

"Nah man, we would've brought our own beer and hid it behind the tent. They're rookies," Jameson adds.

"Truth," I say, offering a fist bump in agreement. "So, what'ya say boys? Looks like we have some celebrating to do." The guys turn to me in agreement. High fives and congratulations are exchanged to both Ben and Jameson on their big days.

There's no bartender minding the beer and wine, but Taylor and his date have been lingering a bit near the bar, keeping an eye on it and making sure it stays stocked. Probably because whatever isn't used is going back to Country Road with Taylor. I pop open beers for everyone, and Landon lines up some shot glasses as the girls approach us.

On instinct, I pull three beers from the bin but pause and put one back looking at Ashton. She smiles in appreciation as I grab a bottled water for her instead.

"Thanks, Owen." Her eyes glisten, and she bats her hand in front of her face. "Sorry, hormones. Apparently, I cry a lot when I'm pregnant. Oh," she gasps, "that's the first time I've really said it out loud. Wow, guys. We're going to have a baby." She looks around at our group, and we all raise our bottles in a toast to the new addition to our crew.

Shots soon follow, and we stand around talking like

it's just any other Saturday night with our group of friends. I suppose in many ways it is. We're just a new version of who we've always been. And we're dressed much nicer than usual.

The DJ switches up the music a little and some older dance music fills the tent. The girls are dancing in their spots where we stand. Drinks in hand, swaying together, and laughing. Then Ashton stops mid-spin and stares at the dance floor, mouth agape, a look of horror in her eyes. The girls see her and stop too. Eventually all of us turn our attention to what is happening just a few feet away.

"Ah hell, what are they doing? Someone's bound to break a hip."

We all laugh at Ashton's comment. It's almost as if she didn't mean to say it out loud because she blushes slightly and shrugs her shoulder. I know she means her parents and family members, but they aren't old by any means. We stand and watch for a few minutes as the dance floor fills with the older crowd dancing, arms in the air, singing along to the music, and having what looks like the time of their lives. One of the aunts must have heard Ashton's remark because she dances her way over to where we're standing and dances dramatically in front of Ashton who playfully pushes her, laughing.

For the next few minutes, several of the aunts and uncles repeat the move and soon the girls have joined everyone on the dance floor. When a song I'm not very familiar with comes on, the older crew spreads out creating two lines facing one another. It looks like a line dance but the music most definitely isn't country so I'm not sure what's happening.

I look to the guys, and they all look equally confused. "Uh, what the fuck is happening?" Jameson asks. We all shrug but take a few tentative steps toward the rest of the crowd. Suddenly, one at a time, they start dancing down the aisle of people. Some of the uncles are doing a little shuffle, but the aunts seem to be really into it.

Ashton pulls Jameson toward her and puts her hands on his hips, encouraging him to dance. Piper does the same to Ben, but he doesn't need encouragement and starts dancing on his own. Landon is with us but standing off to the side a little, not really interested in what we're doing. Minnie grabs my hand.

"Oh my gosh! It's a soul train line! We have to do it!" She's shouting and looks so damn excited I agree without knowing what the hell she's talking about. It's only when I'm pushed in the middle of the aisle of people that I realize I'm supposed to dance. Alone. To music. Dear Lord. I decide to follow suit with the uncles and just shimmy my way to the end before scooping Minnie up into a kiss.

"Are you having fun, babe?" I ask while nibbling on her neck.

"Hmmhmm so much fun. I love you, Owen."

"I love you too, Minnesota. But I'm not doing that dancing shit again."

We both laugh and I know the reality is, I will. I'll do anything this woman asks me to because seeing her happy is my new mission in life.

Chapter 22

Landon

While my friends are dancing and making asses of themselves, I'm struggling to pull my gaze away from the brunette standing off to the side of the tent. I don't remember seeing her here earlier, but she did walk in and immediately hug Taylor. Of course. Women flock to that guy like moths to a flame. I get it. He's mysterious and rides a motorcycle. Women think that bad boy image is hot. I blame all the books with half naked dudes on the covers. Where's the good guy in a flannel? Or the guy dancing with his girl *fully clothed*?

I learned all about "hot alpha" males when I borrowed Piper's eReader one day to look something up. I was floored when her screen filled with nothing but abs. She explained all the different genres of books she reads, and I swear by the time she started saying words like "billionaire alpha Rockstar romance" I had checked out. But, the concept lingered in the back of my head.

Maybe I should take my mom up on her offers to play matchmaker. I mean, I give the ladies a chance and engage in conversation. Heck, I've taken a few out to appease my mother. But, that's been it. None of them have caught my eye. Honestly, the only woman to catch my eye in the last year was Lexie, the bartender at Country Road. That was until I misinterpreted her friendliness for flirting and asked her out. Turns out, her girlfriend isn't into her dating other people.

Whatever, I have too much going on anyway. I just bought a house, moved my workshop from my parents' barn to my own small garage, and am working a lot. A relationship, or even dating, isn't necessarily high on my list of priorities even if the single life is boring and some nights, lonely. Speaking of my workshop, I'm glad Jameson and Owen helped me bring my wedding gift in to the house earlier and hang it. I knew it'd be perfect in Piper's library space and I was right.

When I started working with wood years ago, I never expected people would want to purchase my art pieces. The occasional desk or shelf, sure. But, the art? That was never something I considered. I struggle accepting money for the pieces and prefer to gift them to people instead.

"What's up Landon? Need a beer? I just added a few of those IPA's you like." Taylor pulls me from my thoughts with his question, and I nod. I'm still looking in the direction of his date and feel like an ass, but I can't seem to pull my gaze from her. The brunette looks toward us and catches my eye. She doesn't smile and neither do I.

Seconds tick by and we're both just staring. I feel the cold beer drop water on my hand as I turn my attention back to Taylor and accept the bottle from him.

"Why's your date standing over there, man?" I ask, flipping my head in the direction of the woman across the room who I note has stepped away from where she was standing and is headed for us. Great. She'll probably tell Taylor I was staring at her and he'll kick my ass.

"What?" he asks before the woman steps up next to him.

"I think I'm going to take off, this was a mistake." I note a hint of sadness in her voice.

"I'll walk out with you, I think I'm about done here. I just wanted to make sure they had enough on ice before I leave. I should check in at The Road before too much longer." His tone is calm, and I don't think he's realized I was perving out on his date.

I stand there awkwardly waiting for Taylor and his date to finish their conversation. When he turns to me, I'm taking a long drink from my bottle as he begins speaking.

"Oh, I'm a dick. Hey Landon, this is Addison. Addison, Landon."

I pull the bottle from my lips, and with the back of my hand, wipe a drop of beer that's dribbled onto my chin. I look to Addison and extend my empty hand in greeting. "Hello, Addison."

"Addy, please."

"Addy. You don't feel like staying and dancing? I'm sure you can convince this guy," I say, thumbing toward

Taylor who is now pulling on his leather jacket.

Addy smiles and giggles rolling her eyes. "Not likely. I don't know anyone and feel awkward. I should get home anyway, I have a long drive tomorrow."

I want to ask her more questions. I want to know where she's going, why she didn't drive here with Taylor, why she's into the bad boy thing, and mostly I feel a compulsion to ask her to dance.

"It was nice meeting you, Landon. Tay, I'll see you at your house?" she asks, and my hopeful bubble bursts.

"Yeah. I'll probably be late, though. Just leave a light on for me, would ya?"

Addison nods her head in agreement and sends me a quick smile before hurrying out of the tent in the direction where the cars are parked. When they say timing is everything, they've never been more right. And, whoever "they" are can suck it.

"Ugh, I hate that she's like that." I look at Taylor. Okay, glare at Taylor, but I'm stopped short when I see him holding the back of his neck with one hand, his head thrown back in frustration.

"Like what?" I ask, keeping my tone neutral.

"Shy, embarrassed. Fucking broken. Her dickhead ex keeps screwing with her head, and it's killing me." This is the most random conversation, but I listen as Taylor takes a deep breath and looks at me. "I told her never to marry him. Hell, my parents told her not to marry him, but she did it anyway. Stubborn as a mule that one."

"Your parents? You've known her a long time?" I ask thoroughly confused.

"What? Of course, I have, man. She's my sister."

Taylor shakes his head like I'm not making any sense before saying goodbye and walking out of the tent.

His sister. Not his date. Well then, maybe "they" aren't such bastards after all.

Chapter 23

Ben

"Are you sure you set the alarm?" Piper shouts from the other side of the bathroom door.

"Yes, dear," I shout back.

We've been married about seven hours now, and I promised her I'd stop responding with "Yes, wife." For the rest of the night. It's our wedding night, I don't plan on doing a lot of talking. It's been a perfect day, and tomorrow we'll hop on a plane for a long day of travel to Costa Rica. When we were planning our honeymoon, my only requirement was Piper needed to wear a bikini most of the trip. I'd prefer her naked, but I know that's not reality.

Yes, I'm a horny bastard but, in my defense, if you were married to Piper Law—Sullivan—damn, that has a nice ring to it—Piper *Sullivan* you'd want her naked too. Sullivan. Piper is a Sullivan now. And, my wife. Fuck, I'm a lucky son of a bitch.

I hear the lock on the door click and know Piper is pausing before she opens the door. She whispered to me earlier she was nervous for tonight. I didn't understand what she meant then. We've been together over a year and living together for ten months. Besides all of that, we've known each other our entire lives. We aren't strangers.

But, lying here in our bed, waiting for my *wife* to enter the room, I get it. I understand the hesitation, the nervousness, and the underlying tension. Sure, it's sexual tension but the reality is tonight will be different. We've made love, we've fucked, we've had quickies, and we've had long drawn out session of multiple positions and a lot of orgasms. We can thank whiskey for those last two times. Tonight, we come together as husband and wife. Tonight, we solidify our commitment to not only each other but our future.

The door opens and Piper's silhouette fills the doorway. With only the dim light from my beside lamp illuminating the room, my breath hitches. As she takes a step into the room, I note she's wearing a short white silky slip with only lace covering her amazing breasts. The sides are cut high with more lace trim on the slits. Piper isn't very tall but standing there, her legs look a million miles long.

"Fuck," I croak. Piper smiles and takes a few more steps toward my side of the bed. I shift so I'm sitting on the edge. Standing before me, she takes my breath away. I place a hand on her hip, sliding it down her perfect ass, and along the smooth silk of the slip. "Baby, you look beautiful."

My hand reaches the hem of the silky fabric, and instinctively, I slip my hand under the material to her thigh, tugging her toward me. She gasps and then giggles before catching herself from falling. With her hands on each of my shoulders I raise my eyebrows suggestively.

"Mr. Sullivan, are you inviting me to bed?" she taunts with her breasts in my face, begging to be released from their lacy captors.

"Why, *Mrs.* Sullivan, I believe I am."

With one more tug, I pull Piper toward me and flip her over onto her back. I'm hovering over her, holding myself up on my forearms so I don't crush her. I stare at her whiskey eyes and remember when I looked into those beautiful eyes just over a year ago. I knew then this woman was something special. Piper slides her hands slowly down my arms until they reach my waist. I didn't bother with boxer briefs or pajama pants after my shower so my erection is not contained. A huge smile appears on her face as my dick jumps in response to her dragging her fingers up my back.

"You're beautiful, Piper." She tilts her head to the side and assesses me for a minute. I see her eyes dance with mischief and then she opens her legs more so I settle between them.

"Thank you, Ben. And, thank you for today. It was perfect." Her hips rotate as she speaks. She knows what she's doing is driving me insane but she lies here perfectly calm like her heart isn't beating in tempo with mine. As if I'm not inches from slipping in her wetness and fucking her.

"It was perfect, and I'm happy you're happy," I say, tugging the top of her slip so her hard nipple pops out inviting me to lick it. To suck and tug until Piper gasps and throws her head back. Yep, we're done talking.

I pull the hem of the slip up until her stomach is exposed. I'm glad we're on the same page tonight, and she's foregone panties. Slowly, I slide down her body until I'm nestled between her legs, her pink lips welcoming with her glistening juices. I've been in this spot numerous times in the last year but tonight, tonight is the first time I make my wife come with my mouth. I love having firsts with Piper.

She's wound tight, and I think for a minute she was right when she said tonight would be hotter if we didn't sleep together for a few nights. I feel my dick growing, if that's even possible. I could probably come myself just from listening to her mewl as I lick and tongue fuck her. I feel her orgasm building as she grabs my hair with her hands, and seconds later she's riding my face as her bliss takes over. Placing a few kisses to her inner thigh, I rise to sit back on my knees.

Looking at Piper with her eyes closed, her hair a messy halo above her, I am overcome with quick emotion. This is our life. Moments like this. Pure unconditional love with the one person in this world who loves me exactly how I am. Piper is the woman who encourages me and pushes me to be more. Building a life with her is everything I never knew I wanted.

Piper opens her eyes and looks in mine. I raise a brow and she smiles before pulling her slip off and grabbing my arms. Pulling me to her, I kiss her with every emotion I feel and every dream we share.

"I need you," she moans as I thrust into her. God

she's perfect. Perfect for me. We move together in harmony, our bodies in sync, our hearts beating in unison. The only sounds that fill the room are those of our lovemaking. Our breaths are loud, our groans animalistic, and when we come together I see stars. My orgasm seems to go on for what feels like minutes and when it finally ends, I look at Piper. She's staring up at me with nothing but love in her eyes.

I never expected one night at the local bar to change my life. I never expected a single kiss to change it all. I'll be grateful every day for the rest of our lives for our forever.

The End.

Stay tuned for Landon and Addy's love story.

About the Author

Andrea Johnston spent her childhood with her nose in a book and a pen to paper. An avid people watcher, her mind is full of stories that yearn to be told. A fan of angsty romance with a happy ending, super sexy erotica and a good mystery, Andrea can always be found with her Kindle nearby fully charged.

Andrea lives in Idaho with her family and two dogs. When she isn't spending time with her partner in crime aka her husband, she can be found binge watching all things Bravo and enjoying a cocktail. Nothing makes her happier than the laughter of her children, a good book, her feet in the water, and cocktail in hand all at the same time.

Other Books by

andrea johnston

Life Rewritten

Spring Break (Phoebe & Madsen Part 1)

COUNTRY ROAD SERIES:

Whiskey & Honey (A Country Road Novel – Book 1)

Tequila & Tailgates (A Country Road Novel – Book 2)

Martinis & Moonlight (A Country Road Novel – Book 3)